The Law in Crossroads

Jack Bonner, former lawman, bounty hunter and fast gunman has settled in the small town of Crossroads, Texas, wanting nothing more than to retire his gun and to run his livery business.

When a rogue gunman shoots up a saloon in the middle of the day, Bonner feels obligated to investigate as there is no lawman in town. In an ensuing argument, one outlaw dies and another is taken in for bounty.

Bonner reluctantly agrees to temporary marshal duties until former ranch foreman Barry Dodson takes the job. Things go sour when Z Bar ranch owner, Horace Davies, hires a known gunman instead of cowboys in an effort to turn the Z Bar into a haven for outlaws.

Jack Bonner and Horace Davies are at odds for control of the town. When Davies offers a reward for his demise, Jack Bonner goes into action. . . .

The Law in Crossroads

J.L. Guin

A Black Horse Western

ROBERT HALE · LONDON

© J.L. Guin 2015
First published in Great Britain 2015

ISBN 978-0-7198-1708-3

Robert Hale Limited
Clerkenwell House
Clerkenwell Green
London EC1R 0HT

www.halebooks.com

The right of J.L. Guin to be identified as
author of this work has been asserted by him
in accordance with the Copyright, Designs and
Patents Act 1988

Typeset by
Derek Doyle & Associates, Shaw Heath
Printed and bound in Great Britain by
CPI Antony Rowe, Chippenham and Eastbourne

Viewed from a distance, a visitor to this part of the country, used to the vastness of the prairies, might not even know it was a town. The low, brown clumps of the grassy plain might have been another group of hills common to this country. It was the town of Crossroads, in west Texas, located on the southeastern edge of the Llano Estacado.

Crossroads started with the high hopes and ambitions of Dean Phelps who erected several new buildings to accompany an old stage depot. The man mistakenly believed that the railroad would run their tracks through the region and the location would make a good stop over. The railroad, however, routed their tracks fifty miles north and bypassed Crossroads.

Despite the setback, the quiet community was beginning to attract new faces. The town began to grow in population and new businesses opened their doors. At times, others with no thought to peacefulness came to town.

'Well, now, lookie here,' Cleevus Flaggan said while crossing his wrists over his saddle horn.

Off in the distance, he could see the buildings that made up the town of Crossroads. He and partner Ben

'Stick' Stickney had been riding all day from the miserable camp they had made on the flats to the south. They did not have any camp supplies or much money to buy any. Their hopes were to run across a traveller and take whatever that person might possess. So far, they had not seen a soul in their northward travel on the Texas plains. The two had pulled rein a half mile away from Crossroads and sat in their saddles while wondering about the town.

After their last train heist near Fort Worth Texas, the two thieves had fled with $5,000 of loot to Lajahara, Mexico, southeast of El Paso. For the last few months, they played cards and fooled around with the cantina's women while drinking tequila from early on until very late at night. The men freely spent their money and thoroughly enjoyed themselves; that was until the money finally ran out.

Stickney was the first to wake up when Jose Ramos, the cantina's owner, poked a shotgun barrel to his side.

'Señor, you must go; we grow tired of you!'

Stickney stumbled from the room into the cantina. Cleevus Flaggan, with a shotgun to his back as well, tittered on unsure legs where he stood in the cantina. Both men were rumpled and sick from the previous night's activities. Neither man was armed, their six-gun rigs held in the hands of a third, cross-looking Mexican who stood nearby.

Stickney ran a hand through his thick greasy hair then plopped his hat on his head. 'What the hell's going on, Cleevus?'

Cleevus swept his eyes to the two shotguns nudging

him and Stickney, then he shrugged his shoulders. 'Hell, I'd say we've overstayed our welcome. You got any money left? I ran out last night and a certain *señorita* wasn't any too happy about it. It looks like she called on Jose to collect.'

Stickney shook his head. 'I got some pocket change; nothing to speak of. I was hoping you had enough to hold us over.'

Cleevus looked around at the two men who held shotguns on them. He finished stuffing his shirttail into his breeches then held a hand to the door. 'What the hell, Stick, I guess the party is over. I'm tired of goat meat and beans anyway. Let's go.'

Cleevus looked to the man holding his and Stickney's six-gun outfits and held out his hand. 'We'll be needing our guns.'

'Bring your horses by when you are leaving town; we will put them in the saddle-bags,' Jose said.

Cleevus nodded, 'I get ya, Jose. I got no quarrel with you. We'll be leaving soon as we get our horses.'

The men walked out of the cantina into the powdery dust street. Cleevus kicked in frustration at a skinny mongrel dog looking for a handout that wandered too close. 'I ain't got nothing!' he yelled at the dog.

Taking a cue from the dog, Stickney declared, 'I'm hungry.'

The two men had enough change between them to buy tortillas and coffee from a pushcart vendor. Stickney sniffed the unknown meat contents, curled his nose, then shrugged his shoulder and crammed it into his mouth, wolfing it while Flaggan winced at the

7

rancid taste of the strong coffee.

After picking up the horses, they rode to the cantina but stayed in their saddles. Jose and the other man stood out front, still wielding the shotguns while another man put the six-gun rigs into each man's saddle-bags.

Jose stood grim-faced. He waved the shotgun barrel as if pointing the way out of town. '*Adios, señors.*'

Once out of sight of the cantina, Flaggan and Stickney pulled their horses to a stop to retrieve their six-guns and strap them on.

Flaggan checked the loads in his six-gun and found it had been unloaded. He cursed then filled the cylinder with loads from his gun belt. 'I ought to go back and ventilate that bastard.'

Stickney's head jerked towards Flaggan. 'Hold on there, partner, I kinda like Jose, besides we might want to come back here again sometime. It ain't his fault that we run out of money. We just gotta pull some jobs before we're welcomed back.'

Flaggan remained sullen and silent as he mounted. The men turned their horses north where they could get back to familiar country and do what it was they did, which was thieving.

While gazing at the buildings ahead, Stickney put a meaty dirty finger into his mouth and worked out a stale quid of tobacco from his cheek. He flung the gob away then took a pouch from his shirt pocket for a fresh wad.

'What place is this?' he asked.

Cleevus shrugged a shoulder. 'Beats the hell out of me. The last time I was through this part of the country, there wasn't a damned thing here but an old stage depot and a few farmers. It was a chore to get water and grain for my horse. Now it looks like a whole town has sprung up. It takes money to build a town. Let's go check it out, maybe we can find a golden goose egg in there.'

Ben Stickney gave a thoughtful look at the town. 'It would be good to get a meal and a glass of whiskey, but what if there's a lawman there?'

Cleevus snapped his head around to his partner. 'You worry too much, Stick, we ain't been across the border for nearly six months. If there happens to be a badge-toting law dog in this little burg, he would most likely be a fat old man with a hand that fits a beer mug better than the handle of a six-gun. Hell, it looks to me like the place needs a little livening up and we're just the two that can do that!'

Cleevus gigged his horse forward.

Crossroads was formerly a stage stop between Midland and El Paso, Texas. When enterprising Dean Phelps came in on the stage one day, which had stopped for a change of horses, he liked the looks of the area and the location with plenty of creek water nearby. There were already some homesteads and what looked like the makings of a ranch nearby. He figured that with the proper prodding, the railroad in its progression from Fort Worth to El Paso might make a swing through this section of the country from Big Spring to Fort Stockton, then eastward to El Paso and

9

that would make the location of what he had in mind an ideal spot to locate a rail town.

Phelps immediately went about appropriating property, then began erecting a hotel as a drawing card. Soon, others attracted to the new community by some advertising that Phelps had arranged, saw opportunity. Some who came began putting up buildings as well. Inside of a year, a saloon, a mercantile, an undertaking parlour, and a blacksmith shop as well as a few homes were constructed and Crossroads came into being.

Of the residents that called Crossroads home, Jack Bonner, the owner of the newly opened Jack's Livery was included. The man was fifty years old, of medium height and weight. He had brown hair touched lightly by streaks of grey. A few crow's feet tugged at the sides of his hazel-coloured eyes, otherwise his face had rugged, sharp features and showed only faint age lines beside his mouth, over which he had a drooping moustache.

Bonner was a former lawman turned bounty hunter. He had first laid eyes on Crossroads months ago while chasing a wanted man. A lot of water had gone under the bridge since that day. He'd captured Joe Snipes after a shootout, right there in the Crossroads saloon, then remained in town while the wanted man's wounds were seen to.

In his brief stay, Bonner began to like the looks of Crossroads and the inhabitants. In the days after capturing Snipes, he became friendly with a number of townsmen. Bonner had gained a reputation as a man with a fast gun while serving as a deputy marshal or deputy sheriff in a number of the rowdy cow towns of Texas and Kansas. Law work paid little and a reputation as a fast gun paid nothing, so he gave up law work and turned to bounty hunting in order to profit from his skills.

Bounty hunting had worked out well for Jack, in that he always got his man. He'd built up a nice savings account from the bounty money he had received and began having thoughts of buying a little spread so he could retire his gun. His living in cold camps while chasing men all over creation had lost its appeal. No one in this part of western Texas knew of his past or his fast gun prowess, so Jack began to think that Crossroads might be a good place to stay for a while.

Things changed when local print shop owner, Iver Faulk, wrote a story about Jack Bonner's capture of the wanted man, Joe Snipes and sold it to a Midland, Texas newspaper. The editor of the paper, hungry to sell papers, had knowledge of *Lightning Jack Bonner*'s past reputation with a six-gun. He in turn wrote an enhanced story about the fast gunman now residing in the small community of Crossroads some fifty miles away.

The result was that a few days later, young Billy Quaid, seeking a six-gun reputation, tracked Bonner to Crossroads. When Quaid called Bonner out with a challenge, Bonner, instead of proving his six-gun quickness, saw fit to chastise the youthful man instead.

'I only draw my six-gun for money. Tell you what though, if you scare up fifty dollars I will draw against you,' Bonner said, then turned his back and walked

11

away. He was sincere in his hopes that Quaid would go away and forget about any challenge for bragging rights. Quaid, though not happy, did leave town.

That confrontation, though strange, brought about a proposal from hotel owner Dean Phelps and three other Crossroads business owners who had witnessed Bonner's dismissal of Billy Quaid. The men were desperate to attract business to their newly built town. They had come here and erected their businesses on the false assumption that the railroad would lay the tracks making Crossroads a stopping place, but it was not to be. The railroad bypassed Crossroads, stationing the nearest railroad terminal fifty miles to the north in favour of Midland. The plans and dreams the merchants had of getting in on the ground floor and booming new business seemed all but lost. The town of Crossroads was slowly dying for lack of commerce.

The four townsmen offered to advertise and supervise fast draw contests between Jack and any takers. The challenger would have to pay fifty dollars to draw against Jack. The winner would receive the money. The real money, however, was available in side bets if placed correctly. The business owners, of course, would benefit from the business brought to town by those who would come to witness the contests. The hope was that others might choose to settle in or around Crossroads and grow the community.

Bonner's first thought was to reject the idea, wanting to put his past behind him. Upon further consideration, the scheme held a potential to make a lot of money quickly without having to chase men all over creation for the bounty on their heads. He could lounge around in the comforts of a hotel, enjoy restaurant cooked meals and saloon whiskey, and let the challengers that took the offer seriously come to him.

To his way of thinking there would be but few takers, if any, who would bother to travel to this remote place so his time in Crossroads would be almost like a vacation with the townsmen paying his bills. It would also be a surefire way to make some easy money on side bets. All he had to do was outdraw those that stepped forward. Any man who came forward to challenge his gun prowess would most likely be a misfit anyway, deserving of some delayed justice. Jack Bonner was not in the least worried that someone could possibly beat him to the draw; no one ever had. Jack accepted the offer.

The only dissenting voice to the proposal was that of Lucille Rankin, a middle-aged widow. Lucille was a part-time hotel worker and town nurse when called upon. Jack had come to know and like Lucille while she cared for his prisoner, Joe Snipes. Later Bonner and Lucille had begun seeing each other until Lucille found out about the advertised contest. She walked into the saloon meeting place and verbally protested the contest and chastised those involved. No one wanted to listen to her complaints so she stormed off in a huff; the relationship between her and Jack had cooled.

When the contest gained notoriety in distant newspapers, things went well for a time and the town filled with reporters and onlookers eager to see the outcome themselves. After his billing as 'Lightning Jack Bonner', there were more men coming to town who wanted to take a crack at him than he ever cared to think about. The first challenger was a man seeking revenge for an episode in Bonner's past as a lawman. Another was merely seeking fame and an enhanced reputation. Jack quickly disposed of both challengers.

When a stagecoach came to town, Bonner learned from the driver that the stage line that had given up on Crossroads was now going to begin to make the town a regular stop again and needed a depot. Jack went into action with the idea to set himself up as the new depot/livery operator. He quickly bought the old rundown previous depot with the idea in mind to house a depot for the stage and double as a needful livery for the town.

When the next challenge came, Jack faced a young man who appeared out of character. He was much too young in Jack's opinion to die in the street. Nineteen-year-old Clovis Blanchard had made a challenge in another man's name. Jack learned that the man who hired Blanchard to stand in for him was seeking revenge for a previous encounter when Jack was wearing a badge. Jack did not want to kill the youth, fig-uring Blanchard was acting out of desperation of hard times and tried to talk him out of the duel. When Blanchard persisted, Jack purposely placed a shot to the young man's shoulder, with the intent to wound rather than kill. He then arranged and paid Lucille Rankin to care for Blanchard.

That showing of human kindness was enough to

bring Jack and Lucille back on speaking terms. After lengthy talks and pressure from Lucille to quit the contest and promote his new livery business, Jack agreed it was time to put an end to the contests.

In the meantime, Billy Quaid, the young gunman whom Jack had chastised and run off, returned and plunked his money down for a chance to draw. Jack sighed; he had not had the time to announce the end of the contest to the men promoting the affair. Good for his word, Jack agreed to this one last shootout but proclaimed to all that this would be the very last duel. He was retiring his six-gun and would not participate any longer.

When the final duel was set to take place, it became a botched contest at a crucial moment. The sheriff of Midland rode into town and recognized a six-gun shootout about to happen. At a distance, he fired his own six-gun into the air to get the men's attention. Quaid mistakenly thought it was the signal gun for the draw to begin. He drew and fired his weapon while Jack waited for the actual signal gunner, who normally stood on the boardwalk midway between the two contestants. The signal gun remained silent. The results were that Jack fell to the ground severely wounded.

Bonner had gained a reputation with a gun, even his near death would never change that. Getting himself shot was something he'd learned to take in his stride long ago that was a part of the life he had chosen for himself. He tried not to dwell on something that could happen to those who lived by the gun, in some cases it occurred sooner than they thought. In Jack's mind, he lived in the west, and if a man got himself called out, he either met the challenge or left town. And he did not have it in mind to leave town.

While treating Jack's wounds, Lucille Rankin had taken him into her home so that she could care for him. Jack was bedridden for two weeks before he took to moving around some and regaining his strength. The two had rekindled their courtship with a proclamation by Lucille.

'Your gunfighter days are a thing of the past, Jack. Wouldn't you like that?'

Jack nodded in agreement. 'I've thought about it many times but a man can't run from his past.'

'No, but you can change, Jack. If anyone comes to town looking for you, all you have to do is the same thing that you did the first time Billy Quaid challenged you and you refused to draw. The way to ensure that is to quit wearing a gun to start with. Nobody is going to shoot an unarmed man.'

Jack nodded but Lucille was not finished talking. 'Crossroads is your kind of place, Jack, a good place to call home. You're fifty years old and I'm not getting any younger either but you've got the opportunity to make something good here, what with the livery business and all. Besides, you now have responsibilities to take care of, namely me and then there's Clovis too.'

Jack had plans of putting Clovis Blanchard to work in the old rundown stage relay station he had bought. If the depot and livery worked out, there would be more than enough work for both he and Clovis to handle. It seemed like a bright future for an ambitious man.

It was now six months later. With the stage coming to town twice a week, new folks moved in or close to town and new businesses had developed. Crossroads now had a branch of the Midland State bank and two hotels, all owned by Dean Phelps. A new barbershop opened up by Stan Oldham, and an apparel shop for both men and women owned by a single woman named Mimi Diggins had come to town.

There was a second saloon, named The Way Station Saloon, owned by Cyrus McKinney. Cyrus had come to town just as the shooting contests had begun and operated the saloon out of a tent. He did well, even after the crowds had disappeared, so he decided to stay in Crossroads and had a new wood-sided building erected.

Jack Bonner's new business, Jack's Livery, was doing well. Clovis, in a matter of weeks, had convalesced enough that Jack hired him to help rebuild the rundown depot and livery long before Jack's wounds healed. Business was good and the workload was heavy so Jack also hired seventeen-year-old Bobby Higgins away from Harry Simms, the undertaker. Harry did not mind as the funeral business had slowed to a halt when the contest ended. Harry kept busy, making a new bar for Cyrus McKinney and other jobs such as cabinet making for the arrival of some new homes.

It was a bright, sunny morning. Jack was whistling when Lucille walked up to stand beside him as he was forking hay to the horses in the corral. 'You sound happy, Jack. I'm so glad to see that for a change.'

Jack set the pitchfork down then cut her a glance.

'It's a nice feeling,' he said with a cheerful smile. 'Good to feel like a normal fella with a business and a good woman at his side.'

Lucille looked at him. 'Do you think it's really over, Jack?' She was referring to Jack's past reputation as a fast gunman and to the men who had challenged him to gun duels.

Jack shrugged. 'It's hard to say, but it's been six months since anyone's been around. Most think that I died. Best to let them think it.'

Lightning Jack Bonner was becoming just Jack Bonner again. He discovered that there was more to life than mere survival. In his storied past, there were those who wished to see him dead. Many had taunted him, hounded him in a test of his six-gun prowess and eventually forced him into a lonely life of chasing after wanted men for the bounty. Jack did not believe that he was destined to be a loner forever, denied the opportunity to enjoy more than mere survival by means of his six-gun. He had taken on the six-gun duels for the money involved but then when he and Lucille Rankin got together by circumstance, things began to change for the better. Jack developed a different attitude and sought to settle down and become a business owner.

Jack had been living at Lucille's rental ever since his wounding six months ago. He could have moved out long ago but Lucille had never hinted that he do so. The two got along fine and cared for one another but neither had mentioned marriage. The social buzzing of sinful living had died off after a few weeks and the couple were accepted as a pair in town.

Jack wasn't sure that he could fit into the 'husband' mould, doing the right thing in society's demanding eyes. He'd never been married, though close twice before but each time he had moved on. The life which he had led was rough by eastern standards but this was the frontier, the west where the land gave little to those who lived in it; you compromised to accept things the way they were or you left. Previously, Jack would not compromise his employment or his way of doing things in order to settle into married life and become someone's clerk, so he chose to leave behind any relationships.

Using what skills he possessed, Jack had chosen to become a lawman, then later bounty hunting. During that time, he had learned to respond instinctively to danger in order to survive, at times, forced to kill without compunction in order to preserve his own life. The school of experience was all that Jack Bonner had to fall back on. The time had now come that Jack wanted to put the gun aside and live a sedentary life. The past six months of living with Lucille while recuperating from his injuries had been pleasant. It allowed him to rebuild the old livery into a viable business without the use of his six-gun.

Lucille had told Jack of her having been married previously and how she had suffered an abusive relationship. Her former husband left her to participate in the War effort. Any thoughts of a reconciliation evaporated when the man died in a wartime skirmish. After the War, Lucille came west to make a new life for herself. She and Jack did not dwell on their pasts, choosing instead to make do with what they currently had and were satisfied with each other's station in life.

When Cleevus Flaggan and Ben Stickney walked their horses into town, all eyes were looking up and down the street.

'Everything looks new,' Stickney said.

Flaggan pursed his lips. 'Looks that way. Let's get a drink and check things out.'

They nosed their horses to the tie rail fronting The Way Station Saloon. The two dismounted, tied their reins then stomped the boardwalk and went through the batwings of the new building.

Cyrus McKinney stood behind the bar, cleaning glasses from last night's business while his wife Dixie was sweeping the floor, when the two men came in. Cyrus looked up expectantly. Dixie glanced at the trail worn men but didn't make eye contact.

She was not in complete agreement of Cyrus's choice of businesses. She'd just as soon he had put his energies into a dry goods business of some sort; something more respectable than a common saloon. She almost never came around, not wanting to be thought of as working there, the exception being to bring Cyrus his lunch on a regular basis. Once there, she would help out with the cleaning of the place. The couple had grown accustomed to occasional strangers stopping in ever since the stage had begun its run through town twice a week some six months ago.

What was unusual was the looks of the men. They

were both dusty and rough-looking with six-gun holsters tied to thighs. Cyrus, in the past, had seen plenty of men like these two and he got a sinking feeling in his gut, knowing they spelled trouble.

'Good morning, gentlemen, are you looking for a drink?' he asked tentatively.

Ben Stickney rested his hands on the bar, and nodded. 'Is the beer cold?'

Cyrus chuckled. 'Mister, at this time of year, nothin's cold in these parts but it's about as cold as you'll find this side of the Colorado Mountains. It's a nickel a glass.'

Stickney nodded then plunked a hand full of change on to the counter. 'We'll start with a coupla beers and a bottle. Whyn't you have the little lady bring them over to a table for us?' He then turned and walked to a table.

Cleevus Flaggan hesitated for a moment. 'You got any lunch fixen's, boiled eggs and such? We ain't eaten for a time.'

Cyrus nodded. 'We got some baked beef and bread leftovers from last night. Dixie will bring it over for you.' Cleevus nodded then went to the table where Stickney dropped into a chair and slouched. The men swigged the beer then began passing the whiskey bottle back and forth.

Later, Dixie delivered the two drinking men their third beer and bent to take away the used glasses, when Cleevus reached over and hooked an arm around her neck, extending his hand down to cup one of her breasts. He stuck his head over her shoulder next to

21

her ear. He grinned, showing a mouthful of tobacco-brown teeth. 'Darlin', how about you come over and sit with us?'

He breathed a fetid whiskey and tobacco breath into her face while reaching his other hand to the hem of her skirt. Dixie, horrified at the move, fought to slip out of the man's exploring grasp then put a hand to her mouth and nose and quickly stepped away out of his reach.

'You go to hell, mister!'

'Where you going, sweet thing?' Cleevus called as he made a grab for her but Dixie was quick and turned away with a hand to her mouth, repelling a retch.

Cyrus watched while Dixie scuttled away to the safety behind the bar.

'Did you see what that filthy man just did to me?' she hissed at Cyrus.

'My wife doesn't work the floor,' Cyrus announced, hoping to calm the situation. 'She's just here helping out with the cleaning.'

Cleevus Flaggan stood; he was slender of frame and looked to be quick. Gun confidence had given him an arrogant tilt to his head that spoke of nothing but trouble and the liquor had helped that along as well.

'I don't allow a woman to be rude to me,' he spat out. 'Fact is, I don't like it at all!' He then drew his six-gun and shot two quick shots into the bottles behind the bar.

It was mid-afternoon when the two pistol shots rang out from down the street. Jack Bonner flinched as he stood

22

behind the counter of his livery, stage depot. His hand dropped instinctively to his hip even though he was not wearing a gun. Years of relying on his six-gun had ingrained that reaction and old habits were hard to die. It was unusual someone would be shooting in town, especially this time of day. The last shots sounded previously during the day were the two that had put Jack on the ground some six months ago.

When two more shots rang out, Bobby Higgins looked over. Jack shrugged.

'I guess I'll go see what this is all about.' He reached under the counter and pulled out his gun rig, a rolled up cartridge belt and holster with a .45 Colt inside. He hadn't even had the rig on for some time now, finding it a hindrance while working around the place. Jack strapped on the rig then pulled the .45 and checked the loads. He spun the cylinder, dropped it into the holster.

Jack stepped out of the livery building when Lucille Rankin rushed up to him. 'Jack, what are you doing? You can't! You're retired,' she said breathlessly.

Jack stopped. 'I'm just going to see what the trouble is about. No need to get panicky; nobody has called me out.'

Lucille knew he was right; somebody needed to see to the shootings. Still, she was apprehensive about Jack going out with a gun on his hip. She could not suppress the knowledge of what he was capable of doing or the fear of what the outcome might be.

'Do you have to take a gun, Jack?'

Jack flashed a glance in her direction. 'Somebody

down there just used a gun, most likely for an unsavoury reason. It seems to me, if I look into the matter, that a gun might come in handy.'

It was hard for Lucille to stifle further comments but she had said all she could without upsetting Jack further. She stood aside and Jack walked away.

Up the street, a hundred yards away, the two horses stood hip shot in front of The Way Station Saloon. As Jack walked along, he put a hand to his six-gun, picking it up then letting it drop back into the holster. He knew there could be trouble inside but it did not worry him, though anyone else would wonder if he still possessed a quick hand after all this time of being idle, not even practising.

Jack put a hand to the butt of his six-gun as he pushed open the batwings. In his peripheral vision, he noticed Cyrus standing wide-eyed with hands held shoulder high behind the bar. Jack swept his eyes to the table on the right where a slim man stood with his gun out and the other, a beefy man, remained seated with a smirk on his face. Jack stepped inside to stand close to the bar while facing towards the men.

Jack knew their kind from the times he had worn a badge. He'd seen plenty of men just like them all over Kansas and Texas; roughshod lowlifes too lazy to work and now they had whiskey under their belts. They were two misfits out of place. He knew from experience that the only way to treat them was with authority to his voice.

'Too early in the day for raising hell,' Jack said. 'Holster that six-gun and settle down!'

Cleevus Flaggan jerked his head towards Jack. 'Well

24

now, what have we here?' he snickered to Ben Stickney.

Flaggan took a half step so that he now faced Jack but did not advance any further. Neither of the men made an effort to move.

Jack, noting the rough looks of the strangers, let his thumb cock the hammer of his Colt but made no move to draw it. He was as prepared as he was going to get for whatever was to come.

'Are you a marshal or something, mister? I don't see no badge on your shirt front,' Cleevus said. 'Not that badges mean a whole lot to us one way or the other.' He grinned then cast a glance to Stickney.

'We don't have a marshal right now,' Jack said in a resolved tone. 'My name is Jack Bonner. I'm a citizen of Crossroads and I'm speaking on behalf of the whole town. We're used to peace and quiet and would like to keep it that way. You'd do well to holster that six-gun. Maybe Cyrus here could give you some coffee before you regret your actions.' He quieted while waiting for Cleevus's reaction. When all he got in return was a scornful glare from the man, Jack decided to put more authority to his voice and demand what he expected of him. 'Since you're not responding to logic, I want you to know that I ain't asking you politely and I won't say it again.'

'Oh I see, Mister Jack citizen of this criss-cross hole,' Cleevus said with a sarcastic twist to his voice as he snickered drunkenly, 'and what if I don't?'

Jack remained solemn-faced, staring intently at the man. 'Then your partner will have to go get the under-taker to carry your body out on a board and make the arrangements,' he replied, his voice steady and low.

Stickney's snickering came to a stop. Cleevus straightened his stance. 'Then I reckon I'd better do as I'm told. I surely don't want to get carried out on a board by no undertaker.'

Stickney set up straight, casually letting his hand fall to his gun handle. 'Sounds right to me.'

Jack wasn't buying this feeble act. He knew what was about to happen.

'Good then,' he said firmly, as if going along with the charade. 'Holster that six-gun and let's all go our own way.'

'Whatever you say, mister citizen,' Cleevus said while casting his eyes to Stickney. Cleevus dropped his six-gun into his holster. 'There now, how's that?'

Jack had not raised a six-gun towards a man for six months. He hoped he hadn't lost his edge. He supposed it was something akin to riding a horse, something a man never forgot how to do but he could get rusty from non-use. Six months was a long time for a gunman to go untested but there was no reason or occasion to draw the gun in retirement. He wouldn't be standing here now except for the fact that there was nobody else in Crossroads to keep the peace so he figured it was something he needed to do. He had hoped this matter would settle without serious bloodshed but deep down he knew that was a fantasy.

He felt the tension in his trigger finger. In his mind there was no question that he was as fast as ever and he had no doubt about the outcome that was about to happen.

With his six-gun now holstered, Flaggan just stood silently glaring at Jack as if waiting for him to make the first move. Stickney remained seated while glaring as well.

Flaggan broke the silence first. 'What'd you expect us to do now?' he asked snidely.

Jack was quick to answer. 'Now you and your friend will get out of here and leave town!'

'Uh uh.' Flaggan shook his head. 'We ain't paid for our drinks yet. You go on now, mister do-gooder, before we get riled. Go on now before you get hurt.'

Jack knew the man would draw his six-gun at any time now. He glared at Flaggan. 'I think you've had your chance. I'm done talking.'

Flaggan's eyes widened, telegraphing that he was drawing his six-gun.

In a lightning draw, Jack's six-gun came into his hand then roared. Flaggan's six-gun stopped its upswing from his holster and dropped from his hand as the impact of the .45 bullet hammered into his chest. Jack swung the muzzle a few inches to the right and blasted a beer mug off the table where Ben Stickney sat. Stickney was in the middle of making a clumsy draw of his six-gun when the mug disintegrated. He let go of the handle of the six-gun as if it were on fire. The gun clattered to the floor while Stickney propelled his hands up, palms out.

'Don't shoot, mister!'

Jack stood for a moment, staring at the man while letting the gun smoke float off. 'I could have shot you easy,' he said.

27

Stickney nodded. 'I can see that now but I . . . I don't want no part of this! Cleevus drank too much, he ain't eaten much over the past few days. He was feeling his oats, what with the whiskey and all. We didn't mean no harm. Now you've gone and kilt him.'

'Didn't mean any harm, huh? You sat there egging him on to shoot up the place, then figured to draw down on me without saying a word! Cyrus,' Jack called over his shoulder, 'pull out that greener and cover this one while I get his gun.'

'I've already got him covered, Jack.'

Jack gave a quick glance to see that Cyrus did have the shotgun pointed at Stickney.

Jack walked over then picked up Stickney's six-gun and stuck it in his waistband. 'Cyrus, I've got him covered now so go and see if that other one has any life left in him.'

Cyrus lay his shotgun down, walked from behind the bar to Flaggan's side and reached a hand to the side of the man's neck, feeling for a pulse. He shook his head. 'He's done for.'

Jack bobbed his head. 'Figured.'

Dixie McKinney came from behind the bar, where she had been crouched, while placing a hand to her forehead. Her eyes were wide open, staring in unbelief. 'You just killed that man, Jack!' she exclaimed.

Jack eyed her. 'When a man is drawing down on me with killing on his mind, I don't have time to study his reasoning; I do what I just did. I killed him before he could kill me. It doesn't get any simpler than that.'

'But you are known for the fast draw,' Dixie bleated.

Jack nodded. 'And I wanted to put that behind me; killing a man for no reason other than defending a fast draw reputation. It appears to me that you and Cyrus may have been in a world of hurt had this thing gone any further. What were you going to do, just let him do as he pleased, tear the place up then stick a gun in your face; maybe put a bullet hole in you or Cyrus?'

Cyrus held a hand out in an effort to calm the situation. 'We are not ungrateful, Jack.'

Dixie frowned. 'The killing just seemed so damned unnecessary. . . .' Her voice trailed off.

'Did you hear me ask them to leave town?' Jack asked.

Cyrus nodded. 'That we did, Jack. You're right, you gave them their chance.'

Jack turned to Stickney. 'Who are you and what are you doing here?'

Stickney swallowed hard. 'Name's Ben Stickney. His name was Cleevus Flaggan. We were just passing through and thought we'd get a drink and some food.'

'Where you from and where were you going?' Jack asked as he wiggled the barrel of the six-gun around for emphasis, never swaying far from centring on Stickney.

'We've been down to Mexico and were heading home.'

'Where's home?' Jack asked.

'Texas,' Stickney answered.

Jack chuckled. 'Texas kinda covers a lot of territory. You want to know what I think? I think you and your partner were in Mexico all right and most likely laying low from doing some jobs in Texas. Your money ran out and you were on your way back to do some more jobs.'

Stickney sat blanch-faced. 'Well, we were a little short on funds, that's for sure. Spent the last of what we had for the drinks.'

Jack swayed his head from side to side. 'No money to pay for the burying?'

Stickney shook his head. 'I guess the county will most likely take care of it.'

'The county doesn't owe him a free burying,' Jack noted. 'Crossroads has an undertaker, though. Maybe he will take care of your friend for whatever price his horse and goods will bring. We'll see.'

Stickney tried to smile but couldn't make his face do it. 'Does that mean I can go? I mean, I didn't do any of the shootin' or anything. You must have heard me when I agreed with what you said about going our own separate ways. I got a ways to go and. . . .'

Jack cut him off. 'Any dodgers out on you and your partner?'

Stickney gulped, casting his eyes around as if looking for a saviour. 'I don't think so,' he said unconvincingly. When Jack did not respond, Stickney rephrased his answer. 'I meant to say that Cleevus had the one out on him that I know of.'

Ben Stickney then lowered his voice. 'There might be one out on me but I'm not wanted in this part of Texas and that's the God's honest truth.'

Jack almost chuckled; funny, he thought, how a grown man would resort to referring to the Lord when he was in a tight fix but the rest of the time, he went on doing whatever he pleased without regard to his maker. 'Are you a church-going man, Ben?'

Stickney squirmed in the chair. 'Well, I uh, used to go with my sister; our ma sent us almost every Sunday, course that's been a while ago.'

Jack nodded. 'Well, Ben, you want to know what I think?' Before Stickney could give an answer, Jack continued. 'Since you are not sure if the law might have an interest in you, I think you and I should ride over to the Midland sheriff's office and get this cleared up. When we get there, it might be easier on you if you were to fess up to what you two have been up to.'

Stickney's face paled further as he sat in the chair. While he was a big, beefy man, he looked more like a child talking to a teacher or his father in his plea. 'Hell, you got no call to make me go to the law. You ain't no real lawman or anything. You ain't even got a badge that I can see.'

Jack nodded. 'No I don't have a badge but you're going to real jail, that's if there's a dodger out on you. Elsewise, you got nothing to worry yourself about and can ride on home. Just so's you know, I used to do some bounty hunting and right now, I could use a little extra dough for turning Flaggan's body in and bringing you in alive.'

Stickney looked at the floor. 'Well, there is one poster out on me, but I can prove my innocence.'

Jack grinned. 'Good for you, now you'll step out the door and we'll walk up the street to the livery, so's I can get myself outfitted for travel. Keep in mind, Ben, that

31

I will shoot you if you try to escape.' He motioned with Stickney's six-gun for him to get to his feet.

A group of people, which included Lucille, stood outside on the boardwalk when Stickney, followed by Jack, came out of the saloon at gunpoint. Lucille had a worried look on her face.

'Are you all right, Jack?'

'I'm fine; I just have to get this man and his partner's body over to the Midland jail to see the sheriff. I'll take Clovis with me to help stand guard. We'll be gone a couple, three days. Bobby Higgins can run the place while we are gone. I don't believe the stage will be in before we get back.'

Lucille touched Jack's arm. 'Jack, if you take them in then the word will get out and it could start all over again. Everyone will know that you're not dead and some might come after you.'

Jack placed his hand on hers. 'We won't let that happen, Lucille. A gunman won't come looking to gun me down unless there's profit in it or fame. I'm not offering either. This was different; all I did was stop a bad thing from happening. If these two hadn't been stopped and had continued raising hell, then others might get it into their heads to show up and do as they pleased as well. Word gets around quick, particularly amongst no accounts. Sometimes it's best to face the problem head on when it's fresh, before it's allowed to fester.'

Jack walked Stickney to the livery then called to Clovis Blanchard. Clovis came right out.

'Look under the counter, in that box, and bring me

those cuffs I showed you. Then I need you to saddle my horse and yours. We'll be gone a few days, taking this here man to the sheriff's in Midland.'

When Clovis handed the handcuffs to Jack, he in turn handed Stickney's pistol to Clovis.

'I know that you know how to use a six-gun so consider this man dangerous and if he tries anything, shoot him. It would save us a lot of trouble.' Then he busied clamping the cuffs on Stickney's wrists.

'What did he do?' Clovis asked.

'Never mind what he did; I believe that he's a wanted man and there's most likely a bounty out on him and his partner as well. I'd like you to help me watch over him and make the delivery. Their horses are over in front of The Way Station Saloon. Take a tarp along to wrap the other one's body in. I imagine that Cyrus will most likely be glad to help get the corpse out of the saloon. When we turn these two over to the law, it'll be an extra payday for me and you. Then you can buy that line back dun you've been wanting.' Clovis smiled while bobbing his head in understanding, then he turned to get the tarp.

As soon as Jack, Clovis and their prisoner rode out of town, Stickney began jabbering endlessly. 'I need food and drink. I didn't do nothing, so how about letting me go? I'll leave this part of the country and won't ever come back. The reward on me ain't much. Why, it's hardly worth the bother. No need for these cuffs; I won't run off on you.'

Jack did not reply to Stickney's banter as he rode in front with Stickney's horse in line behind him.

Flaggan's horse followed with a lead rope attached to a D ring on the back of Stickney's saddle, and Clovis Blanchard brought up the rear.

It was near dark when Jack pulled his horse to a halt under some cottonwood trees with a middling stream trickling nearby.

'This is good a place as any to make a camp,' he declared.

'Stickney, you go over next to that tree and sit on your butt. You do anything funny and I'll brain you. You try to escape and I'll shoot you. Clear enough?' He waited until Stickney nodded before giving instructions to Clovis.

'Clovis, I'll help you unload the body then if you'll take care of the animals, strip and hobble them so's they can nibble and get at the water, I'll get a fire going for our supper.'

'How far did we come?' Clovis asked.

Jack picked his hat up from his head and ran a hand across his hair before replacing the hat. 'I expect we did fifteen miles or so. We get an early start tomorrow, we'll be in Midland come mid-afternoon.'

It was an uneventful evening in the little camp, other than Stickney offering, 'If you take these cuffs off, I could do some of the camp chores.'

Jack smiled. 'That's mighty decent of you, Ben, but Clovis and I don't mind carrying the load.'

Their evening meal consisted of fried chicken and biscuits, which Jack had gotten from Rosa's Café before they left town. That and a can of beans warmed over the fire made a right fair supper in an open camp. Jack sat supping coffee. He reflected on Midland's Sheriff Willie Hughes. He'd first met the man when delivering Joe Snipes to jail to collect the bounty some six months ago and Hughes seemed to be fair in his duties.

Hughes became aware of the advertised fast gun contest involving Jack that would put Crossroads on the map and let Jack know that he did not approve. If things got out of hand, Hughes figured he would arrest Jack on charges of inciting violence. He didn't do anything immediately because lawfully, nothing had happened yet. Hughes assumed that even if the contest went forward, it would most likely fizzle after one meeting. If either Bonner or a challenger hit the dirt then either man would have received his just desserts.

Later, though, inside a week, the contest did go forward and Jack bested three different challengers. The night before the supposed last contest, Lucille Rankin sent a rider to Sheriff Hughes in a plea for him to come and put a stop to the contest. She was intent on getting Jack to quit trying to throw his life away.

Hughes had rode hard into the night and got to town just as Jack and his challenger, Billy Quaid, were getting set to draw. Hughes fired his pistol into the air to get their attention and put an end to the contest. Quaid mistook the pistol shot for the contest's signal gun, had drawn and fired on Jack. Two shots sounded, resulting in Jack lying in the street, wounded.

Jack did not fault Hughes for the actions he had taken. The lawman was just doing his job. Later, after Hughes made a few visits to Crossroads, Jack found that he liked and respected the man. They were on a first name basis now and Jack was looking forward to seeing the sheriff again.

At 2 p.m. the following day, Jack headed the group as they walked their horses down the main street of Midland. Sheriff Willie Hughes watched from a window when Jack turned his horse in to the tie rail. Hughes, a middle-aged man who weighed more than he could comfortably carry, spent most of his days sitting behind his desk, letting deputies do the legwork. When he recognized Jack Bonner's profile through the window, he got up with a sigh and walked out on the boardwalk to see the visitor.

'Howdy, Jack.'

'Howdy, Willie, I brought you some business. I believe there's a flier or so out on these two.'

Hughes showed surprise at Jack's declaration. 'I didn't know you were back in the bounty hunting business, Jack. Isn't the livery business lively enough for you?'

Jack smiled. 'Let's get this one inside and I'll tell you all about it. You remember Clovis, don't you?' He flared a hand to the young man.

Sheriff Hughes cast a glance to Clovis. 'Yeah, sure. The last time I saw you, you were flat on your back with a bullet hole to your shoulder. You look like you came out of it pretty darn good, Clovis. I'm glad to see it.'

Clovis shrugged a shoulder. 'Jack, him and Lucille took real good care of me and I've about got the kinks worked out of my shoulder. It's almost as good as new.'

Later, after some men hauled Flaggan's body away and a deputy lodged Stickney in a cell, Jack sat in an easy chair facing the sheriff's desk. Jack sent Clovis to deliver the prisoner's horses to the livery and asked the youth to see to the care and lodging of their own animals while there.

Sheriff Willie Hughes finished writing on a pad. 'According to the posters I have, those men are worth $500 apiece from the railroad. They'll be happy the robbers were caught up with. Did they have any of the loot left?'

Jack shook his head. 'As far as I know, Stickney said they spent their last dime on whiskey back in Crossroads.'

Hughes nodded. 'It's easy enough to figure that the stolen loot is spent money after all this time. I'll send off a wire asking for authorization to pay the reward. I think you know the routine, Jack, it'll take a day or so.'

'I still have an account at the bank, just have them deposit it in there.'

'No problem, Jack.'

'Willie, I'd appreciate it if you didn't let on to anyone about who brought those men in. I don't want to give anyone the idea that I'm wearing a six-gun again and have become a target.'

'I was hoping you would say that, Jack. I did not have any interest in letting word out about your involvement in the capture of those men, especially to the newspapers.' He hesitated a moment then said, 'I've been thinking on something, Jack, that I think you ought to consider. Crossroads is growing so rapidly that I believe we need representation there but it's a hard day's ride from here. I ain't too hip on making the ride myself, except of course, in an emergency. The county won't allow me a full-time deputy to be in residence there and a once-a-month showing doesn't seem to accomplish much. Anyone on the prod could dodge him.'

Jack tensed, for he knew what the sheriff was going to say before he even said it. 'I don't want the hassle of being a resident deputy, Willie. I don't have the time or interest to listen to all the complaints that comes with the territory. I gave up law to go bounty hunting, then gave up the bounty hunting under bad circumstances to run my new livery business. That's the way I'd like to keep it.'

Hughes held up a hand. 'Not asking you to give up or change anything, Jack. What I have in mind is a little different. What if I gave you authorization to uphold the law as a deputy but didn't let anyone know but the ones in this room? You just go about your business as usual but you have the support of this office, if or when you have a need. Just like you did by stopping Flaggan and Stickney.'

Jack was shaking his head in refusal but Hughes wasn't finished. 'You don't even have to report to me or anyone else, except when you feel the need to. I believe I can get the county officials to keep their mouths shut; pay you a fair wage as a part-time deputy and deposit it into your account here. It would make a nice little savings account. So no one needs to know but us.'

Jack shook his head again and stared at the floor. When he looked up, he said, 'I didn't need or have any backing when I stopped those two.'

'That's a fact but you are an experienced man, Jack. Hell, you know the law. I think you knew those two were no accounts the minute you laid eyes on them. All I'm saying is that you would have the freedom and the backing of this office, if there ever was a need.'

'Why is it so damned important that you want someone wearing a badge in Crossroads?' Jack asked.

Hughes flared his eyes. 'I think you already know the answer to that, Jack. It would just be a show of law. Without law there's no safety net of justice, no decency. A few no goods could move in and cow the whole town with no one to stop them.'

Jack remained silent.

Hughes sat back in his chair, clasping his hands on the desktop. 'Let me ask you this, Jack, who is watching over the town when you are gone? Are there some men there that would answer a call to arms when needed? I know that even if you were deputized, you still couldn't do it all by your lonesome. It ought to be an agreed-upon community effort, keeping the peace. You and the other residents ought to get together and make a plan. One of these days, there is apt to come the time when something might happen in Crossroads, a robbery or such that would jar the community. By the time this office becomes aware of the problem, the culprits would be long gone.

'If deputized, you would have the authorization to gather a posse. You do not have to do anything for now and it would get the county officials off my back to cover that territory. And I would feel a lot better just knowing someone with your knowledge and capability is there to handle things.'

Jack sat silently; there was logic in what Hughes had said. There could have been a half dozen or so of the likes of Flaggan and Stickney storming into town to do as they pleased. In numbers they would have overwhelmed one man, namely himself, then be free to raise havoc. Since brought to mind, he was actually surprised there had not been more men on the dodge coming through town on their way to and from Mexico. For all he knew there could be a gang in town right now, tearing the place up and no one to stop them.

He shuddered to think of just how vulnerable the citizens of Crossroads were.

Jack needed to roll things around some before making a snap decision. He would go over everything in his mind before making a commitment. In the past, he had no problem being a lawman; he had proved it through years of service. The thing that troubled him was that for the past six months he had been lying low, had hung his six-gun up and was content to operate his business in peace. He had hoped that his reputation as a man with a fast gun had died when he lay wounded in that Crossroads street some six months ago.

If word got out that he was wearing a badge and a six-gun again, then those seeking a reputation or looking to avenge a past encounter might come looking for him again. He did not want to display a badge because of his past and he knew that pinning one on would not fly with Lucille, and she would protest loudly. The two were not married but still he did not want to jeopardize their relationship.

Jack stood. 'I'll let you know in the morning, Willie.'

He treated Clovis to a steak dinner that night before retiring to his hotel room. He spent a restless night, mostly in thought of Sheriff Hughes's offering but managed to get three or four hours' sleep.

After breakfast the next morning, Jack gave Clovis enough money to pay their livery bill and ready the horses while he walked over to the sheriff's office. He opened the door and stepped in. Hughes sat behind his desk, coffee cup in hand.

'Good morning, Jack. The coffee's on.' He then waved a hand to the pot on the stove. 'Did you sleep all right?'

Jack nodded. 'Fair enough sleep and no on the coffee, I've had plenty.' He dropped into the seat of the easy chair facing Hughes's desk. Jack got right to the point of the visit. 'I thought about what you said yesterday and a lot of it makes sense. Crossroads does have a need for law enforcement. When I get back, I'll propose a meeting with the others and see if the town can afford a marshal. That would take the pressure off me.

'Now, as for becoming a part-time deputy, the answer is yes, I'll do it with a few stipulations. You can swear me in and give me a badge but I will not show it unless there is an absolute need to.

'I think you should still send a deputy down once a month for a showing but do not let him know that I pack a badge. Some of those younger deputies do not understand and tend to run off at the mouth to others when they ought to stay quiet. If, by chance, I needed the deputy's assistance when he comes around, I would identify myself to him. Otherwise, I'll either report to you direct from time to time or get word to you when warranted.'

Hughes pursed his lips. 'Aren't you afraid that Lucille would not like the arrangement, Jack?'

Jack shook his head. 'I see no need to tell her of my being a deputy sheriff but after I explain my intent to see that a marshal is in place, I believe she'll be in agreement to that end. If we have a town marshal to take care of things and my services as a deputy sheriff are used strictly as a backup to the marshal, then those on the prod are not apt to come to town just to try me out.

'To most folks' way of thinking, including the news-paper editors, Lightning Jack Bonner's fame faded into the sunset. Those with any interest believe that I died or just gave up packing a six-gun, so there is no reason for anyone to come around to challenge me. If, however, word got out that I was packing a badge and a six-gun, then everything Lucille and I have worked for in the past six months would be reversed and we'd be right back where it all began. It has to end sometime and I don't intend to be lying in the street with a bullet in me again.'

When Jack returned to Crossroads, he told Lucille about Sheriff Hughes's suggestion of having a meeting with the business owners of the town and coming up with a candidate to become the marshal of Crossroads. He did not mention the fact that he swore an oath and became a part-time deputy sheriff nor did he show her his badge, which he kept under a flap of his saddle. Jack figured it would be better to remain quiet rather than listen to Lucille rant.

Lucille was receptive to the idea. 'That would be great, Jack, having a full-time marshal to patrol and take care of things so that you wouldn't be compelled to rush out every time a gun is fired.'

Jack nodded. 'I did tell the man that I would act as a back-up to the new marshal as I'm sure most of our other citizens would do as well.' Lucille did not respond so Jack let the subject drop.

Two days later, Jack sat at a table at The Crossroads Saloon while waiting for the merchants of Crossroads and others to assemble for the ten o'clock meeting. Melvin Hines, owner of the saloon, placed a pot of coffee and several cups on the table before Jack.

'They ought to be here any time now, Jack.'

Dean Phelps, owner of the two hotels and financier of the newly established branch of the Midland State Bank, complete with new manager Aaron Reason, came in and went to Jack's table.

'I invited Sweeney and Roach to come to the meeting, Jack. They don't own a business in town but the two of them can use a shotgun as needed.'

Jack nodded his head in agreement; the two beer-guzzling handymen usually kept busy building or repairing things for Phelps or others and doubled as gravediggers. By arrangement, the two men had stood guard over the contestants while the shooting was going on. Jack liked both men and knew that they would be good back-ups for whoever became the new town marshal.

Seated at one table was Z Bar ranch owner Horace Davies who had recently purchased and headquartered his sizable ranch three miles north of Crossroads. Davies's right hand man and ramrod for the Z Bar ranch, Barry Dobsen, sat next to him. Dobsen, along with most of the Z Bar crew, were holdovers from the previous owner.

Jack wasn't surprised by Davies's appearance at the meeting, even though the man had not established a business in Crossroads yet. That's not to say that he hadn't tried. Davies arrived in town three months ago and had apparently arranged to purchase the former Nickerson ranch from Tom Nickerson's widow Evelyn. Mrs Nickerson, a former New York socialite brought out west, had never really shared her husband's enthusiasm for ranch life.

After Tom Nickerson's death, the result of a fall from a horse, the woman had tried to adjust but not being a woman of the west, she found that continued running of the ranch was overwhelming. It became her desire to dispose of the ranch then return to her native New York. She immediately put the place up for sale.

If a sale did not happen quickly then her plans were to instruct Barry Dobsen to round up the cattle and drive them to the nearest railhead. When done, she would pay off all the hands and close down the ranch while waiting for an eventual sale. Folks began to figure something was in the offing when the stage delivered a short, balding, suited and vested thin man to

Crossroads. The man looked the part of a lawyer, which later proved to be true.

When the stage arrived, Evelyn Nickerson was there to greet the new arrival, then the two went immediately to her residence. A day later, Davies came to town and booked a sleeping room as well as a conference room at the hotel. It was there that Evelyn Nickerson and her lawyer, Avery Bartleson, negotiated a deal with Davies. Bartleson offered the Nickerson ranch complete with livestock included. A working ranch had considerable higher value than starting all over again. A consideration that was beneficial to the seller as well as the buyer.

Evelyn Nickerson, by an agreement with Tom, had moved from the ranch into a rather nice home, which Tom had built in Crossroads long before his death. When Evelyn had determined that she was not suited for ranch life, she had made it clear it was either living in town or she would go back to New York. Tom split his time between the home in Crossroads and the ranch.

Evelyn was a prudent woman and in no hurry to leave Crossroads after Tom's death. She intended to sit tight until his holdings had been disposed of in a manner that would ensure her financial future.

No one was privy to the details of the agreement between Davies and Mrs. Nickerson; perhaps Dean Phelps the bank owner knew but did not divulge any information. Horace Davies made several less than viable offers for the ranch but the woman and Bartleson held out until they received the desired considerations.

Davies, in the meantime, in an apparent attempt to gain some sort of control in the area, took the time to visit every business owner in Crossroads, including Jack Bonner. Davies did not take long to make it clear that he had sufficient cash to buy the livery, if Jack was interested. Jack, just as other business owners in Crossroads, went into business with the purpose in mind of building their future in Crossroads and was not interested in moving on.

Jack's only reply to the man's veiled offer was, 'I'll keep in mind that you have an interest if I decide to move on, Horace.'

Davies nodded. 'Fine little town here, Jack. I intend to be a part of it. One thing that stands out is the lack of available women. The boys out at the ranch have to ride all the way to Midland if they get the urge for some female companionship.'

'That's a fact. Crossroads doesn't have sufficient business as yet to entice any loose women to take up residence. The gambling and rough housing that generally go with a house of ill repute hasn't caught on. Not enough money circulating to sustain that kind of activity, I suppose.'

'That could change someday, if the right man had control of one of the saloons.'

Jack watched as Davies walked away. To Jack's knowledge, no one had taken Davies up on his offers, though it was rumoured that Davies financed, perhaps owned a share of the new mercantile store operated by Willard Shaw.

Davies, a round-bodied, silver-haired man in his

mid-fifties, did not look the part of a rawboned working ranch owner. His appearance was more that of an eastern financial man, perhaps a dealer in real estate or banking. He always wore a business suit complete with vest and dangling gold watch chain. The man, though friendly, came off as being a bit pompous in his dealings. It was evident that he bought his way through his activities and was used to those in his employ carrying out his orders without question.

Harry Simms the undertaker walked into the saloon followed by Iver Faulk, print shop owner and publisher of the local *Crossroads Gazette*, a one-page news flyer put out once a week. Abe Wilkins the blacksmith came in, and behind him came Carlos Santos of Rosa's Café. Jackson Riles, Crossroads's mercantile owner, who dealt mainly in food and clothing, was there and his competitor, newly arrived Main Street mercantile owner Willard Shaw, who dealt in dry goods, horse tack and farm implements was there as well. The two men did not share the same table.

Jack waited until the men had seated before he stood to address them. Most had a coffee cup before them except the two town handymen, Ike Sweeney and John (Roach) Crane who each had a mug of beer in their hand.

Jack had already glanced around the room and mentally checked off each man as he came in. The only business owner who was not in attendance was Mimi Deggins, the apparell shop owner, but Jack saw no need to hold up the meeting on her account. This was men's business anyhow.

He stood and walked to the bar, then turned to face the assembly. 'As you men are aware, two no accounts came to town a few days ago and were in the midst of shooting up Cyrus's place when I heard the shots. I confronted them, and ended up shooting one of them and taking the other to jail. They were both wanted men on the dodge. Sheriff Hughes over in Midland suggested we all get together and hold this meeting. He is aware that his office is fifty miles away and can do little more than pay an occasional visit but that does nothing to stop any future harassment should one occur.'

He paused for a moment and glanced around the room. All the men sat sombre-faced, waiting for Jack to continue.

'Sheriff Hughes asked me a question, just who is watching over the town of Crossroads. That got me thinking that what he said made sense. I am no different from any of you men, in that I own a business here as well. But who is looking out for the store? I mean, what if some trouble comes to town? Who is going to see that it gets stopped before it turns ugly?'

'We got no problem in the way that you handle things, Jack,' Iver Faulk spoke up.

Jack turned to face Iver. 'I took care of one incident, so what if another incident had occurred while I was away? Who amongst you would even go and check it out? What the sheriff proposed and I go along with, is to hire a full-time marshal for Crossroads. I might add that I am not a candidate but I would back the man up as I am sure most of you would too.'

Willard Shaw stood up. 'If we agree to hire a marshal, then someone is going to want to collect a tax to pay his wages. I'm against it. That's one of the reasons I came to Crossroads and started my business here, so that I got away from all those taxes that most cities charge to take care of police work and such.' He then sat back down as others were nodding their head in agreement with him while the rest merely glared at him.

Jack nodded. 'What are you going to do, Willard, if someone comes along and robs your store at gunpoint? Are you going to ride fifty miles to get the sheriff or go after the robber yourself? What we need is someone on hand who can stop the trouble before it gets started.'

His remarks started another round of murmuring before Jack cut in again. 'You are right about one thing, Willard, the man's wage has got to come from someplace. If each business put a little into the fund then it would not cost so much for any one of us. You can call it a tax if you want but I do not see any alternative. We need someone on the street, someone who each of us can take our troubles to. That someone will take the time and initiative to smooth over minor squabbles that pop up from time to time, and stand firm when a real problem arises.'

Harry Simms rose. 'You all know that I am not getting rich in the undertaking business. That is why I do carpentry work on the side. Even though money can be tight at times, I am willing to pay my fair share to what Jack is outlining. If we are going to grow as a town then we have to modernize. I say we elect a city council and a mayor to oversee things and that would give the new marshal someone specific to answer to.'

Jack clapped his hands in agreement. 'Very good, Harry, I would vote for you to be on the council. Who could we vote in to become the mayor?'

Iver Faulk raised a hand. 'Everybody knows that Dean Phelps is the mayor, whether he's voted in or not.' The muttering of agreements from the seated men resounded.

Dean Phelps got to his feet. 'I see where this thing is going and I would have to say that I would be honored to act as the mayor, and I believe that each business owner has a say in any meeting so they would all serve as a council. The purpose of this meeting of which Jack has pointed out is for each of us, for our own good, to come together and hire a city marshal. Jack said he was not a candidate but Jack, would you stand in as marshal until a suitable candidate comes forward?'

Jack smiled. 'Hell, Dean, I just did that this past week and took someone to jail.' The audience laughed. 'All I'm saying is that I don't want to do it on a permanent basis. I think things should go along as always, with all of us looking out for each other until a marshal is hired. I just don't want Mrs Nickerson or anybody else coming to me, complaining about someone's dog pissing on her flowers.' Everyone laughed again.

Phelps said, 'Jack, you stood up for Crossroads in its time of need and you've made it plain that you don't want a full-time job as a marshal. I believe that I am speaking for all of us here when I say that just knowing that we can count on you to act in an official manner is enough. We promise not to flaunt the fact that you are an acting marshal while we take the time to advertise and see if a worthy candidate comes forward.'

Jack nodded his understanding.

Harry Simms said, 'Who you going to advertise to, Dean? Most of the male population of Crossroads is right in this room.'

Iver Faulk said, 'I can run a short story in the Gazette so's everyone here and around will know about the need for a marshal and when I go to Midland later this week, I'll get Milton Ayers to put an ad in the *Midland Centennial* calling for applicants. And I won't mention that you are the acting marshal, Jack.' Jack smiled his pleasure at everyone agreeing to be discreet.

Phelps nodded. 'That ought to do it, Iver. All we need to do is to wait until a man showing interest comes by and then we can determine a wage for him.'

'He'll need a place to stay, food and such,' someone said.

Phelps nodded again. 'I'll provide a room over at the hotel and I think between Rosa's and the hotel restaurant, we can see to the meals.'

Carlos Santos nodded in agreement.

'What about an office and a jail?' Stan Oldham asked.

That question caused everyone to start buzzing again.

Willard Shaw, already stung by learning he'd have to pay a share for town marshal wages, stood and scowled.

'This is getting out of hand! First it was wages, now you'll be asking everyone to chip in to build a damned jail. There ain't that much money to be had in Crossroads. Most of the time, there ain't shit going on around here. I've half a mind to sell out and move on!' The man was red-faced and obviously upset.

Phelps said, 'As business owners, it is all of our responsibility, Willard. We won't ask you to do anything other than provide a keg of nails from the back room,' he added in reprimand. 'If some of you would see to the building materials, I'll pay the wages for Sweeney and Roach to erect a jail on that empty lot down near Jack's Livery. It doesn't have to be elaborate, a small room for an office and one or two cells. We can always expand later.'

New Z Bar ranch owner Horace Davies held his hand up. 'I've got a whole crew of men that are used to cutting and hauling posts and boards. I'll have them bring a couple loads in.'

After others had offered goods and services, the meeting began to break up. Jack was satisfied that the ball was rolling and he walked back to the livery.

Lucille Rankin sighed. 'I suppose if you can't shake being known as a former gunman, it is better that you take care of the lawman duties in Crossroads, even if it is only temporary. Perhaps men will think twice and show some respect before they try to kill you, if they know that you represent the law.'

'It changes nothing, Lucille, no one is advertising the fact that I am just filling in and it's only until a full-time marshal is hired,' Jack reminded.

'I hope a good man comes by real soon before another incident happens.'

Abe Collins and Dom Kagel were on the dodge and heading to Mexico. The two had held up a mercantile in Hays City, Kansas and Abe had gunned down the proprietor when the man went for a shotgun. Now they were on a robbing spree that had lasted all the way from Kansas, clear through the Indian Territory and into Texas. They held up any unlucky wayfarer that happened to cross their path. It didn't matter to either man who they took from, stage, store, freighters or single traveller, hell, money was money.

The two had not expected a stage to be out here in the middle of nowhere but when the opportunity came their way, they saw no reason to let it go by.

The driver and the shotgun rider were unaware when two masked men rode up from behind the stage headed to Fort Concho. Out of nowhere appeared a bandit on either side, with a six-gun pointed menacingly. The rider, Abe Collins, on the driver's side, fired his six-gun over the top of the men's head and motioned with the six-gun for the man to pull up. With a six-gun pointed at each man the driver had no alternative but to stop.

'Drop that scattergun over the side!' Dom Kagel on the shot gunner's side yelled.

When done, both the men on the topside held their hands up in surrender.

'We ain't carrying a strong box, nothing on board but passengers,' the driver advised.

'Then why the hell you got a shot gunner along for?' Collins scowled.

'Everybody out!' he ordered. When no one complied, a six-gun roared, the bullet smacking through the side of the coach. 'I said out!'

The door flew open and a man tumbled out with hands held high. A second man remained in the coach. 'My wife is hurt. She took that bullet you sent in here! I need to look after her.'

A suited man wearing a derby said, 'Get your ass out here or I'll plug you too!'

The man exited the coach and held his hands up.

Collins slid off his horse. 'Too bad for her, all of you ought to have done as I told you and nobody would have got hurt. Now just so's you know what's going on; this is a hold up. All's we want is your valuables, money, jewels, guns and such. Just put it all in that derby of yours and stand aside. Don't be holding out on us,' he warned, 'my partner Dom is not likely to favour anyone hiding something.'

The bandit stood while the two male passengers emptied their pockets.

'Please, mister, can I see to my wife?'

'I'll check on her,' Collins said, then motioned the two men away from the coach with his six-gun before he stepped into the coach. He looked at the woman's lifeless, white face.

'Too bad, she wasn't a bad-looking ole gal,' he muttered then yanked a gold chain from her neck. He lifted each of her hands and removed a wedding ring, the only other jewellery located. He stepped out of the coach and called to the driver, 'You two come down here and empty your pockets, then open up the boot so we can get a look in the luggage. Dom, keep 'em covered so's they can't jump me.'

'Is she going to be all right? Can I check on her?' Derby hat pleaded.

Collins motioned with his six-gun to go ahead. An almost instant wail came from the coach. 'You son of a bitch, you killed her! I'll see you hang for this!'

The answer came by way of a bullet that brought a yelp from inside the coach.

When satisfied that they had everything worth stealing from the coach, Abe and Dom mounted and rode away swiftly.

The driver knew about where they were on their route to Fort Collins and from his estimation, it would be closer to Midland than to go on to Fort Collins. He elected to drive the stage to Midland, in hopes of getting medical help for his wounded male passenger and to alert authorities of the murder of the woman and the robbery.

At the time of the stage robbery, almost three months had passed by without any takers coming forward to apply for the marshal's job offered in Crossroads. Jack Bonner resigned himself to the fact that he was stuck with the job for now but at least it had been peaceful since the one incident at The Way Station Saloon. The small jail was finished, complete with a tiny tin stove and coffee pot. Jack and Lucille arranged the office with a donated desk, chairs and writing materials, and the front door remained closed as no one occupied the structure.

There was no visible law in Crossroads and that fact made the town a good place for someone on the run to draw on. It was quiet around town but Jack Bonner knew that the calm would not last forever.

As if by premonition, five mounted men rode on to the main street of Crossroads. They rode all the way through town to come to a halt in front of the marshal's office. Jack had spotted the men when their horses had first set hoof to the street. He also spotted the badges on the rider's chests. Something was up, he knew, as he stepped forward to greet them.

Jack recognized the sheriff's deputy Sid Hanford from Midland when the man dismounted and tied his reins to a hitch post. 'Howdy, Hanford, I can't say that I'm happy to see you here in force.'

Hanford nodded. 'I bring news, Bonner, but it ain't good.'

Jack grimaced. 'Is there any other kind? You men all come over to the livery; I have a pot of coffee going. Clovis will see to your animals while you take a rest.'

Once inside the livery office and everyone had a filled cup, Deputy Hanford spent the next ten minutes telling Jack about the murder and robbery of the northbound stage which had come from their overnight stay here in Crossroads.

'It was about twenty-five miles past here. We left town as quick as we assembled. Sheriff Hughes wanted me to make sure we stopped by here and told you of the misdeed. He said that you were now the acting

56

marshal here in Crossroads.'

Jack nodded, grateful that Hughes had not told Hanford that Jack was a part-time deputy as well. 'That's right, I am, and I'll make sure everyone in town is aware of what happened and to be on the lookout for any strangers that come by here. That's if you can tell me what they look like.'

'The bastard that did all the talking is the one who shot the woman then plugged her husband when he went to check on her. From what I was told, he's young, of medium height and skinny, maybe twenty-five or so, dresses in trail garb, and rides a sorrel horse. The witnesses gave no distinguishing markings on the man, just that he has brown hair, a sunburned face, faded red shirt, scuffed up boots. The other one was called Dom, is older, maybe thirty-five or so, shorter than the other, bad teeth, rides a roan horse, dressed like any cowboy whose been on the trail for a time. They say the only time he spoke was to order the shotgun pitched from the coach.'

To Jack, the description given would fit half the cowboys in Texas but he didn't say anything, allowing Hanford to continue. 'By direction, we rode out to where the robbery took place and followed some tracks that led north for a time, then west before we lost them on some hard pan.'

'Trying to throw anyone tracking them off the trail,' Jack injected. 'It's hard to follow a man who is purposefully trying to hide his trail.'

Hanford nodded. 'I figure they're making a run to Mexico and may already be too far ahead of us to matter. They might show up in El Paso or any place they can throw some of that loot on top of a bar. You know from your past experiences as a bounty hunter that those with fresh taken money like to celebrate as quickly as they can. They have at least a thirty-hour head start on us but we intend to keep at it for a day or so, though. I'd sure like to catch up to those two. They're both candidates for a short rope on a scaffold.'

'I'd offer to ride with you but it looks like the five of you ought to be enough,' Jack said.

'We can handle it and I do appreciate the thought, Marshal, but I believe it would be best if you looked out for the citizens of Crossroads in case those two show up here.' The men all shook hands and Jack watched as the posse rode out of town.

He stood in thought for a minute; he knew from experience that what Hanford had said was accurate. Those on the run would want to rest over at the first place they figured was out of reach by lawmen. Crossroads was the nearest place for many miles that would fit their needs, if they even knew of its existence. He was hopeful that the two would bypass the town but in reality, he figured to expect that they could show. With that thought in mind, he strapped on his six-gun then checked the loads. If, in fact, the outlaws did show up, he would be ready for them. Jack strode straight over to Dean Phelps's office and told him of the deputy's visit.

'So you believe that they might show up here even though the men said they were headed south?' Phelps asked.

Jack nodded. 'Nobody knows for sure where they are or where they are headed. It would be best if we spread the word to everyone to be on the alert, especially the bartenders. They need to check their weapons and have them close at hand just in case.'

'I'll see to it, Jack.'

It was an hour past supper time when a knock came to the door of Lucille Rankin's rental. Jack and Lucille were sitting in the living room talking over the day's events. Jack looked as Lucille said, 'I'll see who it is.'

Harry Simms stood on the porch. 'Is Jack here?'

'Yes, he is, Harry, come on in.' Harry slipped past Lucille and stepped hurriedly to stand before Jack. 'Two rough-looking men just rode up to the Crossroads Saloon. They went inside. I peeked in the window and I saw Melvin sweating bullets.'

'What are they doing? Are they harassing Melvin or anyone else?'

Harry shook his head side to side. 'No, they're just drinking but I thought I better let you know. You know, in case it's them.'

Jack nodded. 'Thanks, Harry, I'll check things out. Just in case it is the two wanted men, could you go fetch Sweeney and Roach? Tell them to show up with their scatterguns. They don't need to do anything but back my play.'

'I'll tell them,' Harry said excitedly, then turned to leave.

Jack exhaled. 'And Harry.' The man turned back to face him. 'Take it easy, nothing has happened yet.'

Harry nodded then left.

As soon as Harry was gone Lucille exclaimed, 'Oh, Jack, I hope you don't get involved in another shootout!'

Jack stood and silently stepped to take his gun-belt from a wooden peg and strapped it on before checking the loads again.

'I won't go in until Sweeney and Roach show up,' he said in conciliation. Lucille nodded as Jack stepped out the door.

Only a thin sliver of a moon hung in the star-filled sky. A rustler's moon, was the thought in Jack's mind. Plenty of bad guys on the prod when darkness came and the moon phase didn't seem to matter.

Jack started walking towards the saloon. Sweeney and Roach came to his side when he had stepped half the distance.

'Howdy, men; for now I'm just checking on things; need to see if one of those horses is a sorrel and the other a roan.'

Roach said, 'I saw those two when they rode in but I didn't note their horses. They got that look of riding a long trail. Both of them have a six-gun on his hip and they look rougher than hell. They reminded me of a couple of cowboys on the run. I was coming over to fetch you but Harry Simms got to you first. Ike and I were waiting for you to come out before we came over.'

Sweeney stepped over and walked around both the tied horses. When he walked back he said, 'Both are sorrels, Jack, but they could have switched the roan out by now.'

'Thanks,' Jack acknowledged. 'I want one of you to take position out front here and the other to come in the back way; keep your shotguns at the ready in case any shooting starts but there's no need to cause a ruckus unless they try to give us one.' Both men nodded then Ike Sweeney stepped away down the side of the building to the back of the saloon.

Jack placed a hand to his six-gun then stepped to the building's front; he peered through a window and saw the two men standing with their elbows resting on the bar. When he stepped to the batwings, Jack hesitated only a moment, loosening his six-gun in the holster, before stepping into the lantern light. It was a move he'd done a number of times before when he was lawing in various cow towns. Once inside, Jack took a step over to keep his profile from being silhouetted in the doorway.

Jack swept his eyes around the room. A table to the right held four Z bar cowboys engaged in a card game. Before the bar on the left stood the two men in question as well as two other men, whom Jack recognized as townsmen.

Melvin Hines stood behind the bar; he nodded an acknowledgement when Jack walked over to face him. None of the men standing before the bar paid any mind to Jack's arrival. This led Jack to believe that this could be a false alarm. The two men in question were gabbing to each other. If they were on the prod, they would have already known whenever anyone new came in and have positioned themselves for an assault.

'Everything going OK, Melvin?' Jack asked while

keeping an eye on the two men down the bar a ways.

Melvin Hines bobbed his head. 'Glad to see you, Jack, but I think these two are actually just passing through; said they were looking for work. They look a little rough but they paid for their drinks and have been keeping to themselves.'

'Pour me a beer, Melvin, and I'll go have a word with them. Sweeney and Roach are covering the exits, just in case.'

Jack waited until Ike Sweeney came to stand in the darkened back entrance. Jack took the beer mug in hand and stepped over to the two men in question. He noted the nearest man, who stood at nearly six feet tall and weighed 180 pounds or so. In Jack's estimation, the man was larger than most ordinary cowboys who tended to be five foot eight or so and 140 to 160 pounds in weight. The man on his other side appeared to fit that mould. He noted the closer man's beat up holster housing a six-gun riding high on the same belt that held his pants up. It didn't look like a gun slick's rigging; most likely a single action pistol, the kind most cowboys wore but seldom used, Jack surmised.

'Howdy, men,' Jack said as he took a position to the side of the nearest man, the taller one. Sweeney from his position had a clear view of the other man.

When Jack had spoken, the man jerked his head around with a steely-eyed glare. He had close-cropped brown hair flecked with dust; a severe sun-scarred face and a bushy brown moustache drooping around the corners of his mouth. His jowls and neck were peppered with a two day growth of whiskers.

'Why, howdy yourself, stranger,' the man said while giving a toothy grin. 'Are you local?'

Jack nodded. 'That I am. I own the livery here in town.'

Before Jack could add anything further, the man cut in. 'Me and Clarence came down from Midland. Heard there's a ranch down here called the Z bar that might be hiring. We're both experienced hands and looking for a place to light.'

Jack acknowledged by inclining his head. 'Could be they're hiring. I haven't heard but the ranch head-quarters is only three miles north of here. Barry Dobsen is the man to see, he's the ramrod. It wouldn't hurt for you two to ride out that way come daylight and see.'

'I'm Wade Hansen and this is Clarence Biggs.' Wade stuck out a hand to shake.

Jack introduced himself when he shook hands. 'Jack Bonner.'

Clarence Biggs was the shorter of the two men but also heavier in the chest, giving one the impression that he would be a good man to have on your side in a fistfight. He was trail dusty and held a two-day whisker growth, the same as his partner. Biggs nodded then gripped Jack's hand firmly.

Jack noted that both men had the work-toughened hands a man would possess from handling ropes, cattle and ranch chores. Maybe they were just as Hansen said, a couple of cowboys looking for work.

The three men gabbed for a few minutes, the two strangers directing their questions in an attempt to

THE LAW IN CROSSROADS

gain information about the Z Bar ranch. Jack could offer but little; he recognized most of the Z Bar drovers when they road into town for an occasional drink or tobacco, some he knew by name but had no bad dealings with any of them. He really did not know much about the outfit as a whole. Jack finished his beer then dropped some coins on the bar.

'The next one is on me. Good luck to you.' Wade and Clarence thanked Jack for the drinks as he turned to leave. 'My woman's waiting, I best get along.'

Jack did a head motion to Sweeney to leave then walked out. Once out front, Jack turned to face Roach and waited until Sweeney stepped around to them. 'Just a couple cowboys looking for work. They seemed harmless to me. I expect they'll be gone come morning.'

Jack pulled a dollar coin from his pocket and handed it to Sweeney, 'I appreciate your help. Why don't you two have a couple of beers on me?'

Lucille was pacing the floor with worry when Jack returned. She giggled when Jack finished telling of the two men's intentions. 'Isn't that something? Maybe Crossroads isn't such a bad place after all,' she said.

Things were back to their usual quietness around town for the next three days. That was until Jack picked up Iver Faulk's one-page Crossroads Gazette and read a column that the newspaperman had fabricated. Jack grimaced over what he had just read then stomped away from the livery and headed straight for the Gazette's office. Iver Faulk had some explaining to do.

Jack stormed through the front door. Iver Faulk sat

behind a desk facing the street. He became wide-eyed at the sudden intrusion.

Jack held the paper before him and waved it in Faulk's face. 'What the hell is this, Iver? I thought we all agreed that you would not name me as the acting marshal in Crossroads!'

Iver paled and shook his head from side to side. 'I, I uh, never meant to advertise that fact, Jack.'

Jack cut him off. 'Well, meant to or not, that write up you did about how nice and peaceful things are in Crossroads and how the citizens were hopeful for a new full-time marshal. Nothing wrong with that but then you added that everyone was thankful that Jack Bonner was filling in as acting marshal. If that ain't naming me, then what is?'

Iver's lower lip quivered. 'I guess I fouled up, Jack, I never. . . .'

Jack stormed off. He strode back to the livery then showed the paper to Lucille.

Lucille read the piece then tried to console Jack. 'It may not be so bad, Jack; everybody for miles around knows who to come to for help anyway. Not many strangers come by so the story is not apt to spread.'

Jack shook his head. 'Phooey, a copy of Iver's little paper goes to the *Midland Centennial* every time there's a new one printed. That editor, Milton Ayers, doesn't miss a thing. He's the one who wrote the original story that caused all those gunmen to show up here to start with. If he writes a follow up and I expect he will, then my goose is cooked. We'll know in a week or so, if a stranger comes to town looking to test me.'

When the realization sunk in, Lucille let her hand with the paper in it fall to her side. 'I don't know what to say, Jack. I just hope it doesn't come to that. You can take your gun off, refuse to draw. You can resign as assistant marshal; let Phelps worry about who he can get to replace you.'

Jack had calmed some and he nodded his head at Lucille's recommendations. 'That's a good idea, I think I will go and see Phelps,' he said.

He left and headed towards the hotel where Phelps kept his office.

The two men sat in the office, Phelps behind a shiny oak desk and Jack sprawled in an overstuffed chair fronting the desk. Phelps had a copy of the *Gazette* on his desk.

'It's going to happen,' Jack said.

Phelps frowned. 'Somebody coming here to draw against you, you mean?'

'That's right, now that the word will be spread about. I figure Milton Ayers at the *Centennial* will jump right on the fact that I'm wearing a gun again. He'll dig until he finds out that it was me that brought those men to jail a while back and the game will be on again. I expect any would-be shootists in these parts will come a-calling.'

'But you've not been bothered in the last six months, ever since. . . .'

'Ever since I was left lying in the street,' Jack cut in. 'Everyone figured that I was done for, dead and it's been peaceful since. No one ever considered or expected me to make a comeback. Now that it has been declared in print, I'll become a target again for every reputation-seeking gun-toter in Texas.'

'Are you afraid of the outcome?' Phelps asked.

'I've never been afraid to face any man with a gun!' Jack flared. 'I can still face down and beat anyone who tries; I just don't want to!' He paused for a moment then added, 'For money or otherwise.' His voice lowered in volume. 'When I bought the livery and decided to stay in Crossroads, I wanted my past reputation as a fast gunman to die in the street, just as many thought that Lightning Jack Bonner had. It might be best for all if I just move on.'

Phelps's eyes widened. 'You mean leave Crossroads?'

Jack nodded. 'I don't want to, I like it here but I don't want to be the cause of bringing trouble to town.'

Phelps stood. 'You're the only law we've ever had, Jack, why without you. . . .'

Jack cut in again. 'Without me you wouldn't have had trouble to start with!'

Phelps held his hand out, palm down in a calming manner. 'There wouldn't be a town without Jack Bonner putting us on the map. Jack, you're a good man. Someone will come by to take over as marshal. You can't leave Crossroads. I won't let you!'

He paused for a moment then declared, 'We can have Iver print out an announcement declaring that we have a new acting marshal.'

'What are you going to do, Dean, name yourself?' Jack asked.

'Of course not, but Sweeney and Roach can handle anything thrown at them. They will become the new acting marshals. All we have to do is get information to that effect over to the *Midland Centennial*. We can have the two of them doing some patrols and let this thing die down.'

Jack's facial features calmed a little. 'Sweeney and Roach are good back-up men but do you think they could assume the role of lawmen? Will they even agree to do it?'

Phelps shrugged a shoulder. 'Those men will do whatever I ask of them. I know that they are both handy with a gun. I believe that I already told you that before coming here, Sweeney outdrew and killed a card cheat over in Fort Worth and Roach shot-gunned his own wife and her lover out in the family barn. Plenty of badge wearers have tainted pasts.'

Jack reflected on that, he had known some bad men who had reformed and walked the straight and narrow. He himself was labelled a bad man by some, simply because of his reputation as a fast gun.

Phelps continued, 'And I believe either of those two would not hesitate to pull the trigger, if it came down to it. Neither man is a pushover.'

Jack nodded. 'That's a fact. You'd have to pay them something extra to do it.'

'I already pay them for what they do. I don't think either of them would object to spending a little extra time at the saloons where any ruckus might come about. It will give them the excuse to demand free drinks for their services,' he said dourly. 'Give it a chance, Jack,' Phelps pleaded, 'we'll see that things will work out.'

Jack thought for a moment then pursed his lips. 'OK, I'll leave it up to you to talk with those concerned; Sweeney, Roach, Iver and the rest of the merchants. I'll still back Sweeney and Roach but I want to stay out of the limelight. I don't want anyone running to me with their problems thinking that I am the marshal.'

'Consider it done, my friend.'

For the next few days, things were quiet around Crossroads; it seemed that everyone had accepted the fact that Jack was no longer the acting marshal. Ike Sweeney and John Roach Crane did not make a display of their new assignment but no one questioned their authority.

The only fly in the ointment came when the latest copy of the *Midland Centennial* came to town. Milton Ayers, the *Centennial*'s editor, penned an editorial that named Sweeney and Roach as the new acting marshals of Crossroads. That was fine with Jack but upon further reading, he found that Ayers had not cut him any slack. The article went into a lengthy history of the town's former acting marshal, legendary Lightning Jack Bonner. The article told of Jack's receiving a wound in an arranged gun battle six months previously. Upon his recuperation, the storied gunman had assumed some different role in the town. The story was half a page in length, finalizing with *Jack Bonner is still there*.

The article never mentioned the fact of Jack's desire to retire his gun, nor that he was the owner of the town's livery. The whole thing would give a reader the impression that Jack Bonner was back to his old self and now acting in the capacity of town marshal as well.

Lucille sat blanch-faced as she read the paper. Jack was furious.

'So much for letting things die down,' he cursed.

Jack thought of chasing down Iver Falk and wringing the man's neck; it had to be the newspaperman Faulk that leaked information to the *Centennial* editor and most likely received some payment for doing so. Too late now, the damage was done. All Jack could hope for was that nothing would come of the article.

A week later, just after breakfast, Wade Hansen rode into town and straight to the livery; Jack came out of the building and waited for him to dismount. Jack wondered at the visit. He had not seen the cowboy since the day the man first came to town looking for work. Wade spun his reins around the hitch rail, then stepped forward with his hand stuck out.

'Howdy, Jack, me and Clarence got jobs out at the Z Bar.'

Jack shook hands. 'Why, that's good news, Wade. I'm happy for you. What the heck are you doing in town so early in the morning?'

Wade stood straight and said, 'Mr Davies sent me into town to see if you would come and see him. We had some trouble out at the ranch last night and they're all in a dither out there.'

'What happened?' Jack asked.

'Rustlers; they came late in the night, tried to run off a sizeable herd. There was some shooting going on and one of the older hands, Mel Carlson, caught a bullet but looks like he will survive. Davies asked me to come to town and report the incident to you.'

Jacks forehead furrowed. 'Does everyone at the Z Bar know that I'm not the acting marshal any longer?'

Wade bobbed his head. 'We heard that but Mr Davies insisted that I come to get you anyway. He said he wanted to wait to see you before he made any further moves.'

Jack glared at Wade. 'I can't tell him what to do.'

Wade shrugged a shoulder. 'He wants to see you, is all I know.'

'Did anybody go after the rustlers?' Jack asked.

'Barry Dobsen took some of the hands and was looking for the rustlers' trail; the rest of the men are trying to round the herd back up.'

When Wade had finished, Jack said, 'All right, I'll ride out and see him. If you'll give me a minute, I'll saddle up and ride back with you.'

The two men rode their horses at an easy pace for the three-mile distance to the ranch.

Horace Davies was standing on his ranch house porch, drinking coffee when Wade and Jack rode in. Wade peeled off and headed for the corral as Jack walked his horse towards Davies, who held his cup up when Jack dismounted. 'There's a fresh pot made, Jack, if you care for some.'

Jack nodded. 'Sure, I'd like a cup.'

When the two men had filled cups and sat down in chairs on the porch, Davies turned to face Jack. 'I suppose Wade filled you in as to what happened here last night?'

71

'What he told me was that some rustlers hit your outfit in the night and that one of your men was wounded. He also said that your foreman and others are trailing the culprits.'

'That brings about the reason I asked to see you.'

Jack set his cup on a small table dividing the men. 'I'm sure you are aware that I am no longer the acting marshal of Crossroads; also you must know that the marshal of any town is bound by the limits of the town. The county sheriff's jurisdiction takes over outside town.'

Davis gave a half smile. 'I am quite aware of that, Jack. Once word is given to Sheriff Hughes, I imagine that he will take the report but I don't expect much to happen over it. Oh, he'll send a deputy by to talk to me at some point and in reality there isn't much the man can do. We're kind of isolated out here, fifty miles from the county law. I don't like things taken from me, nor do I want the men in my employ to be harmed. I called you out here for a reason. I have a proposition for you since you have a storied reputation as both a lawman and a bounty hunter. I believe you know what to do in these situations. You have hunted down some of the most ruthless men in the territory and brought them to justice.'

Jack grimly listened as Horace Davies rambled on about Jack's law knowledge, tracking ability and prowess with a gun.

Finally, Davis concluded his lengthy explanation with, 'I'd like to hire you, Jack. We need to nip this in the bud. Send a message to others with wrongful ideas.'

Jack held a hand up. 'Hold on here, Horace, I retired from tracking men and bounty hunting and law enforcement. I run a livery in town, that's all.'

'I'm aware of that fact, Jack, but this is different. I am prepared to pay a worthy bounty to see those men brought to justice. You'll have full cooperation; take as many of my men as you need.'

Jack could see that no matter what he said, Davies did not seem to understand that he had given up bounty hunting for the life he was chiselling out now as a livery operator. Still Jack felt an obligation; as a sworn, part-time deputy county sheriff, though no one supposedly knew of that arrangement, he was compelled to do what he thought was right. He figured that it was a good thing that Horace Davies was unaware of the deputy badge that Jack had under his saddle flap; if so, the man would be demanding that Jack get on the rustler's trail without further delay or compensation.

He said, 'I appreciate the offer of assistance, Horace, but I usually work alone when hunting a man. Who knows, maybe your men will catch up to the rustlers before they leave the area. In the meantime, as a concerned citizen I'll ride over to Midland and report the matter to Sheriff Hughes. Maybe he's got some leads on the culprits operating in our area. I've been aiming to get over that way anyway on another matter.'

The other matter was that Jack wanted to find out if the two stage robbers were ever located or if they had eluded Deputy Hanford and the posse some days ago. The posse had not come back to Crossroads so he assumed they were either still on a cold trail or more than likely had given up a fruitless long ride and went back home.

There was no easy way to end the discussion so Jack offered his hand to Davies.

Davies shook Jack's hand limply. Davies seemed mystified and obviously miffed that Jack did not jump at his proposal or say yes to his offer. His eyes flashed with anger.

'There's a lot of money that can be had by the right man who does what needs doing. My offer of generosity will not stand for long, Mr Bonner!'

Jack gave a half-hearted smile. 'I'll keep that in mind.' By Davies making that last remark, it became clear to Jack that the man had motives in mind other than hiring him to chase down some rustlers. He began to wonder if there really was truth to the claim of the rustling. Perhaps the whole thing was feigned; staged for Horace's benefit in an effort to see if any lawman would do something about it.

The wounded cowboy perhaps tried to foil whatever was going on and paid for it with a bullet to his person. The episode, true or not, gave Davies the opportunity to see if he could buy Jack Bonner's gun. Jack hoped that these thoughts proved false.

Davies wasn't used to having any offers he made to any man turned down, particularly the generous offer he was prepared to offer Bonner. In his anger and frustration he blurted out, 'Well, if you're not with me then you must be against me.'

Jack hesitated at the top of the steps. 'I'm sorry you feel that way, Horace, but I didn't come here looking to go to work for you or anybody else.' He then turned, went down the steps and undid the reins to his horse.

'I'll let you know what Sheriff Hughes intends to do about the rustling attempt,' Jack said as he mounted and rode away.

Willie Hughes sat behind his desk attentively listening when Jack told him the recent events around Crossroads and at the Z Bar ranch.

'You said some of the Z Bar men went in pursuit of the culprits?'

Jack nodded. 'That's what I was told. The owner, Horace Davies, offered to hire me to go after the men responsible, and said he would pay a bounty.'

Hughes raised an eyebrow. 'Do you intend to take him up on the offer?'

Jack shook his head. 'I'm done with bounty hunting, Willie. I gave that up when I bought the depot and turned it into a livery. I'm inclined to believe that the rustling doesn't mean much to Davies; he just wanted an excuse to see if he could buy my gun. On top of that, I became your part-time deputy so I figured you deserved to have a report from me.'

'I appreciate that, Jack,' Hughes said. 'I can still have Hanford ride out and see if the Z Bar men happened to catch up to the rustlers but I wouldn't hold my breath. Rustlers on the dodge can disappear as quickly as they come.'

'They most likely are long gone now. Still, it would be a good idea to follow up and make your influence known. You said you'd send Hanford out. I take it that he came up empty-handed chasing after the stage robbers.'

'He told me they lost the tracks before he even stopped to talk to you, Jack. They stayed out a couple more nights, making a big looping circle in hopes of coming across a trail they could follow but nothing panned out so they came on home. When we first learned of the robbery, we were compelled to check things, so the posse went out but I had little hope of a successful conclusion. If those thieves did not show up in Crossroads, I figure they most likely didn't waste any time making a beeline for Mexico.'

Jack stood to leave. 'I'll stop by the Z Bar on the way home and let Davies know that Hanford will be coming by.'

'I read in the paper that you have a couple of men as acting marshals in Crossroads now. That's good.'

Jack flashed his eyes in Hughes's direction. 'Yes, we had the meeting like you suggested. I agreed to be the acting marshal until a full-time man is hired for the job. I figured that it wouldn't take long for a man to come forward and accept the job but that hasn't happened yet.

'All I really want to do is to act as a back-up to a new marshal. Then the *Centennial* advertised the fact that I was the acting marshal. I didn't want to get it started again that I am available for any fast draw challenge, which I am not, so I backed off. Fortunately, there were others willing to handle the temporary job of marshal. I'm quite serious about putting my gun aside, Willie.' He started to walk away then turned. 'I'll still back the marshals up and be a part-time deputy to you as long as is necessary.'

Jack did not relish reporting to Horace Davies at the Z Bar but he rode into the ranch yard anyway. Davies did not come out to greet him but Barry Dobsen waved from the corrals. Jack walked his horse over to talk to the man.

'Hello, Dobsen, did you have any luck catching up to those scoundrels?'

Dobsen shook his head. 'We never could locate a clean trail to follow but at least they didn't get one head of cattle for all the hell they caused. I've taken the precaution of some extra night patrollers.'

Jack did not bother to dismount, figuring what he had to say would be brief. 'Too bad they got away, I was in hopes that you might have caught up to them. I reported the incident to Sheriff Hughes up in Midland. He said Deputy Hanford would be calling on you before long to get the particulars. I stopped by to let Mr Davies know that.'

Dobsen cast his eyes up to Jack. 'He's not here right now, he left yesterday and took the stage to El Paso. He's got to hire some guns to go after the rustlers, I guess.'

Jack frowned. 'That might be a tall order, considering no one knows the name or looks of any of the ones responsible.'

'He's a hard man to figure at times.'

On a warm afternoon several days later, the sweet peacefulness that Crossroads enjoyed began to sour.

Jack was in the middle of brushing his horse at the livery corral when Jackson Riles, the Crossroads mercantile owner, rushed breathlessly up to him.

'I might have some bad news, Jack,' said Riles.

'It isn't often I get any other kind,' Bonner sighed. 'I'm listening.'

'Late this morning,' said Riles, 'some jaspers rode into town from the south. Three of 'em and a real hard case bunch if I ever saw any. They are over at The Way Station Saloon. They all got tied-down six-guns and the leader, at least the one doing all the talking, is a fella name of Leo Sturgis. Two of them went straight to the saloon but Sturgis came over to the mercantile; gave me his name, said he was well-known but by whom I don't know. He bought some tobacco then began asking questions.'

'And I reckon he learned plenty,' Bonner said.

'Not from me,' said Riles. 'Hell, Jack, all he said is that he heard the famous Jack Bonner was the lawman in this town.'

'Did you tell him that Sweeney and Roach were the marshals?'

'Yes, I did but it didn't seem to faze the man, he just shrugged and asked if you were still around.' Riles glanced to the floor. 'I told him you were retired.'

'Thanks Jackson, I'll go talk to Sweeney and Roach.'

Bonner let out a breath then put the brush away. He went inside the livery and strapped on his six-gun outfit, checked the loads then holstered the .45. If Lucille were here, she would no doubt protest loudly, wanting him to handle things without arming himself.

It was good that she was working over at the hotel today, he figured. There were times when confronting strangers, making one's self an unarmed target, might prove to be foolish. He walked away, in search of Sweeney and Roach.

Bonner wondered about this Sturgis, who the man was and why he had inquired about him. It was most likely not a social call. He hoped for the possibility that Sturgis had asked of him out of curiosity; that Sturgis and his following would just ride on out of town before sundown. Possibly, that would happen but Jack was sceptical.

He found Ike Sweeney, shotgun in hand, standing on the boardwalk fronting The Way Station Saloon.

'Roach is covering the back door,' he informed Jack.

Jack nodded his understanding then asked, 'Have you spoken with those men, Ike?'

'Yeah, me and Roach did; a half hour after they rode into town. They are a tough-looking bunch, I'd have to say that, but the lead man, Sturgis is what he said his name is, said they were just passing through. It was a friendly conversation; he offered to buy me and Roach a beer; said they weren't looking for any trouble.'

Jack flared his eyes. 'Do you believe him?'

Ike shrugged. 'I don't know; but we decided to cover the exits, just in case.'

'Thanks, Ike. I'll just step in and see of their intent. You and Roach might want to stick around for a while.'

Jack did his usual loosening of his six-gun in the holster, left his hand on the handle and stepped to the batwings. Using his other hand, he pushed on through.

He stepped to one side as he allowed his eyes to sweep around the room. The only customers were the three men in question, sprawled in chairs around a table and drinking leisurely. Jack noted that each man held his gun hand close to the six-gun nestled in a low-slung holster at his side. They were unsmiling, shifty-eyed men, perhaps used to never sleeping soundly in case a posse came calling; three sets of eyes were watchful, noting every move Jack made.

There was not much variance in appearance between any one of the three men. They all wore range clothes typical of working cowboys. The difference, Jack noted, was that they just didn't come off as working men. Their clothes, though dusty and rumpled from riding, were newer looking, like a cleaned up cowboy at the end of a trail drive. Their boots, filthy but not all beat up, and instead of deep sweat-stained hats, each man wore one recently purchased. This did nothing for the demeanour exhibited, which was sour, standoffish, whereas most working cowboys were friendly.

The idea that these men made their living herding cattle was about as remote as Dean Phelps the mayor doing a wrangler's job. Everything about them said hard cases as plainly as if they wore signs around their necks. Nope, plain and simple, these men wore six-guns for employment; they were thieves or murderers who squeezed the trigger for money.

Cyrus stood behind the bar, giving a look of surprise when Jack stepped in.

'Howdy, Cyrus,' Jack called out but he never took his

eyes off the three men at the table.

'Hello, Jack, did you want a beer?' Cyrus asked quickly.

'That would be fine, Cyrus,' Jack agreed. 'Things going OK?'

'Yeah, they sure are, Jack. It's kind of quiet actually, just these fellas having a few beers, that's all.' From Cyrus's tone, Jack assumed that he was not exactly happy with Jack's visit.

One of the men at the table stood; his appearance was cleaner than the other two. Perhaps he had freshened up at the last creek crossing. He was about thirty years old, an inch or so taller than Jack and lean of frame. His straggly light brown hair hung collar length and it appeared he had clean-shaved a day or so ago, but still looked as if he were made old before his time, perhaps by the effects of hard liquor.

'You're Jack Bonner?' he asked in a heavy unfriendly voice.

Jack nodded. 'That's right.'

'Heard you pinned on a badge here; my friends and I were travelling by so we figured to swing in and have a look for ourselves.'

'You heard wrong,' Jack said. 'I corralled a couple of wanted men and took them in for the bounty a while back but I wasn't wearing a badge then and I'm not wearing a badge now. I believe that you are already acquainted with the two men who are the acting marshals here in Crossroads.'

'You mean that big oaf out front with the scattergun and his skinny partner out back with one too?' the man asked with a smirk to his voice and a spreading grin.

'I wouldn't sell either of those men short. I believe that they are up to the job. They won't allow this town to become a haven for anyone intent on raising a ruckus.'

'I'll just bet they are; plenty of men around that are handy with a gun.' He let his eye stray back to the table where his two companions sat quietly glaring. 'It's like I said before, we just stopped by to see what a famous six-gun puller looks like. We have no intention of over-staying our welcome.' He hesitated for a moment then said, 'My name's Leo Sturgis out of San Antonio.' Then he quieted, perhaps waiting for the declaration of his name to have an effect on Jack. 'My friends here are Baldy Gibbons and Jug Olsen.'

Jack shrugged. 'Never heard of you.'

Sturgis's face twitched at the thinly veiled insult. To a man wanting his name known as a fast gun, reputa-tion was second only to the speed of his draw.

'You're supposed to be fast on the draw, Bonner, but you don't look like much to me.'

Jack grinned. 'Fast enough to have stayed alive all this time. How much faster does a man need to be?'

Sturgis flashed coyote-like, pale brown-yellow eyes at him. 'You've been very lucky, Bonner. From what I read in the paper, I expected you to be bigger, taller but now I see that you are really quite ordinary.'

Jack smiled. 'The newspapers tend to build a man up; otherwise as you say, I am quite ordinary. I find that newspapers are most useful in the privy, otherwise they are packed full of lies.'

Jack was tiring of the banter. 'Well, Sturgis, tell me, now that you've seen me, did you come to town hoping to catch me at a weak moment and make a public bragging name for yourself?'

Leo Sturgis straightened to full height, swelling his chest, his face flushing with anger then he pointed a finger at Jack. 'If I was looking to plug you, Bonner, it would have already been done. I happen to be selective when I make a move on a man with a respectful audience to watch. You and everybody else will know it when I'm ready to call you out.'

Jack hoisted his beer in his free hand. 'Gee, I can hardly wait,' he said sarcastically. 'Better if you spent a little time thinking if you want to see tomorrow's sunshine. One way to make sure of that would be for you and your friends to ride on out of town. Otherwise, you'd make a nice corpse, Sturgis. You'd look good propped up in a coffin out in front of the undertaker's so's everybody can see your dead face.'

Jack swigged a good portion of the beer then set the mug down heavily; he turned on his heel and stepped towards the batwings.

Sturgis cursed. 'Bonner, you son of a bitch; if anybody is lying glassy-eyed in a coffin, it'll be you! I'd put you there right now but I got bigger fish to fry today!'

Jack kept walking without looking back. He felt butterflies fluttering up and down his spine as if he had a target on his back. He stepped through the batwings but he gambled that gunman's pride would not allow Sturgis to shoot him in the back.

Sturgis was still ranting as Jack walked out of earshot.

Ike Sweeney met Jack out front. 'Sounds like you stirred things up in there, Jack.'

'Might just as well get things rolling. I see no sense in a man beating around the bush about his intent. He's either going to come calling or leave town. We'll see before long.'

Jack walked back to the livery. An hour later, he watched as three men galloped their horses out of town. He wondered at that, why they had not booked rooms for the night. Perhaps they had a camp outside of town.

When the stage arrived on time two days later, Jack watched as the stage pulled up in front of the hotel. The driver climbed down and opened the door. Out stepped one woman, then a second followed by two men. That wasn't such an unusual occurrence, except for the dressing of the female passengers. The women wore brightly-coloured dresses. They sported plumed hats and each waved a gaudy parasol over their heads. From what he observed, even at the distance, Jack could see them smiling and flaunting their brash attire that allowed much cleavage to show. These were soiled doves, if ever he saw one, he figured.

One of the men that came out of the coach was dressed in a light-coloured business suit; he was tall and thin but stood straight. It did not appear that he wore a gun on his hip but could easily have a hideout weapon on his person. A gambler, possibly a pimp as well, Jack surmised.

The other man dressed in a cheap broadcloth suit was of medium height and round in the middle, perhaps a traveller not related to the other three obvious passengers.

The four stood idly by while waiting for their luggage from the stage's boot. The driver pointed across the street to the old mercantile that Dean Phelps had renovated to a second hotel when the fast gun contests were going on. To Jack's knowledge, the converted hotel had seen little business since then but now upon a closer look, he could see a small sign out front declaring *Under new ownership*.

The two men each took armloads of luggage and made their way inside the door of the building.

Jack wondered why he had not heard of any business transactions going on. Not that it was any of his business but he figured to ask Dean Phelps anyway.

Dean was all smiles when Jack came into his office. 'Morning, Jack.'

Jack said, 'I see a sign out front of The Number Two Hotel, says under new ownership?'

Dean sat back in his chair. 'News travels fast. It just became official two days ago. I sold out to Cyrus McKinney. He told me that he sold The Way Station Saloon to Horace Davies and wanted to re-invest in the building but he and Dixie want to stay in Crossroads. Apparently he's turning the place into living quarters for some full-time residents so he won't be competing with the hotel business, I was told. It's OK by me, just means more business for the rest of the town.'

'Did you happen to see the passengers who came in

on the stage?' Jack asked.

Phelps shook his head. 'No, I haven't been out of the office.'

'I thought that maybe you were opening a whore house, Dean.'

Phelps glared in wonder. 'What are you talking about, Jack?'

In two minutes, Jack explained that he had observed the four new arrivals enter The Number Two Hotel.

Phelps grimaced in revelation. 'Damn, I wish I'd been told beforehand.'

Both men knew that this put a new light on things. Sure Crossroads was growing but having professional gambling and loose women available in town would prove a magnet to any man with lustful thoughts for miles around. Word would get out.

Phelps gulped. 'This doesn't add up. Dixie McKinney certainly would not have given her stamp of approval to any such clientele. She had voiced on more than one occasion her displeasure of their being involved in the saloon business.'

Jack thought for a moment. 'This has to be the work of Horace Davies. The man had stated as much to me when he made a bid to buy any business in town. He had said the town was sorely lacking in female com-panions; that under the right saloon ownership, things could change. I guess he means to change the whole town for his own benefit.'

Phelps sat shaking his head in bewilderment.

Now that he knew that McKinney had sold out to the man, Jack figured that Cyrus agreed to stay on and run the place for a while. Only way to find out would be to ask the man.

He stood. 'I think I'll go have a talk with Cyrus,' he said as he walked out.

Harry Simms came up beside Jack as he walked towards the saloon. 'I suppose you saw what I saw? You think those ladies are here to stay?'

Jack shrugged. 'I saw two women and two men go into The Number Two Hotel, Harry. They've broken no laws that I know of. I can't say if they are just visiting or are going to be here for a time.'

'I hope they're staying,' Harry cut in, 'those girls looked pretty good to me.'

Jack cut him a glance. 'They ain't here to give it away, Harry.'

Cyrus McKinney was behind the bar when Jack walked in. The place was empty of customers.

'Howdy, Cyrus,' Jack offered.

Cyrus tried a faint smile but didn't get it done with any sincerity. He then turned his eyes to the glass he was wiping dry.

'Oh hello, Jack; I suppose you saw the new arrivals?'

Jack nodded. 'That I did, Cyrus; figured you could fill me in.'

Cyrus shifted his eyes back and forth nervously, not looking directly at Jack and pretending to concentrate instead on the now dry glass that he continued to wipe.

'It's a simple business deal, Jack, I guess Davies decided to expand the business; the girls and Lang will put this place ahead of the competition. He said it would put Crossroads on the map.'

Jack put his elbows on the bar, indicating he wasn't going away just yet. 'Did Dixie have anything to do with this, Cyrus?'

'She had a say in the matter.'

'And she approves of professional gaming and women on the premises?' Jack asked, unbelieving that the woman would do so.

Cyrus sighed heavily, deciding to come clean. 'It was Dixie that insisted that I take Davies's offer. She never liked the saloon to start with, wants me to get into a less stressful business. Davies owns the place now. I agreed to stay on until the new bartender arrives, which I believe he did today.'

'Does Davies owe you money yet, Cyrus?'

'He gave me a good down payment and said the other would come when the place got on its feet and started showing a decent profit.'

Jack spread the fingers of one hand. 'Never mind the dregs these new arrivals will draw into town, hey Cyrus?'

McKinney put the glass down and wiped his forehead with the rag. 'I had to do something, Jack; she was going to leave me if I didn't take the offer.'

Jack stood. 'Sounds like it's a done deal. I'll let Sweeney and Roach know; I'm certain you're going to be wishing to see them come late one night.' He turned to leave. 'Now you and Dixie will be running a whore house. Did Dixie know that or did she find out when the new residents checked in?'

Cyrus's face blanched. 'She didn't know and neither did I. Davies encouraged me to buy the building from

Dean Phelps. Davies said for me to leave it up to him to keep the place filled and paid for a month's rent in advance. He just didn't tell me what kind of people would be the inhabitants.'

Jack turned and walked out of the saloon and headed back to Phelps's office. Inside the room, he slouched into a chair.

'So McKinney sold out to Davies and was encouraged to buy Hotel Number Two from you, which he did. I don't think you or McKinney understood what Davies had in mind. Davies now has a hold on Crossroads. He owns controlling interest in the Z Bar ranch, The Wayside Saloon, and I suspect he has a stake in Shaw's Mercantile and Cyrus McKinney's new hotel.'

Phelps was quick to respond. 'I made my deal concerning the hotel with Cyrus. Horace Davies had nothing to do with it.'

'That may be true but I believe that Davies can manipulate Cyrus McKinney to do as he wants. Cyrus's new housing is dependent on Davies providing the residents, which happens to be The Way Station Saloon workers. The question is, how many more businesses does the man have a finger in? How much more before he has control of the whole town and makes it the kind of town he wants instead of the town we've come to build on? What problems we have in Crossroads were few until Horace Davies showed up and I can't say that his intentions are all that honorable.'

Phelps sat for a moment before answering. 'I never looked at it like that, Jack. I suppose he could make life miserable for some of the competing merchants. He could force his employees to shop at Shaw's Mercantile and put Jackson Riles at the Crossroads one out of business. The Way Station Saloon could play havoc with Melvin Hines's Saloon; put him out of business.

'Davies never asked me about selling out to him but then maybe he figures that he doesn't need to. I still own the buildings that house Iver Faulk's *Gazette*, Stan's Barber Shop and Mimi Diggins's dress shop. That only leaves Harry's undertaking, Rosa's Café and Abe Wilkins the blacksmith and yourself as independent owners. With enough influence, the man could vote himself as mayor and hire whomever he wants as a marshal.'

'It's a consideration,' Jack said.

Dean Phelps cursed then said, 'I thought all along that Davies was in this with us. Here, we're trying to calm things down and put a marshal on the street to keep the town quiet, and he goes and upsets all the planning!'

'Well, those new additions will not entice me to spend any time or money at The Way Station Saloon. Could be that enough Crossroads citizens and surrounding residents will see things as I do and simply stay away. It won't take long for that gambler and those women to move on if they don't have enough customers to extract money from.'

'I hope that you are right, Jack, but I wouldn't count on it. Most of the men around here, including me, take a trip up to Midland whenever their urges get the best of them but others either don't like that arrangement or even bother to plan ahead. Damn! This puts things in a new perspective. I'm not sold on the fact that Sweeney and Roach will be able to handle things; after all they are not actual lawmen. Hell, knowing them, they might just join in the fun!'

By the next morning, almost everyone in Crossroads knew of the new arrivals and the banter on the street was heavy with question and criticism. The town had remained quiet last night but then word hadn't had time to spread as yet. It would take a day or so, Jack figured, then the community would be subject to change from quiet and peaceful to what many thought they had previously left behind in order to settle here. While many, such as Harry Simms, perhaps living in lonely bachelorhood, could only see the excitement that the new arrivals generated. Other residents knew the debauchery and violence that came with gambling and prostitution would have a negative effect on Crossroads.

Within a week, a transformation began to take place in Crossroads. Melvin Hines closed up Crossroads Saloon early evenings for lack of customers while The Way Station Saloon came alive, every table taken. Just as Jack had figured, the soiled doves were the drawing card to bring visitors to town. The Number Two Hotel now sported the name of The McKinney House, its doors opening and closing at all hours of the night with clients arm in arm with a dove. Dixie McKinney, distraught over being suckered out of the saloon business into running a whore's house, couldn't take it anymore. She caught the northbound stage out of town, leaving Cyrus to the mess he'd created. Rosa's Café changed their operating hours to accommodate hungry late night revellers. Jack's Livery and Phelps's Hotel – along with the other businesses in town – depended on daytime activities and were not susceptible to any notable change.

Sweeney and Roach were no longer seen in the light of day doing carpentry work, instead busied in the evening hours keeping drunks from wrecking the saloon and other buildings. A few six-guns fired into the air by over exuberant drinkers brought the acting marshals on the double. So far, they had deposited four different men into the jail for overnight holding. At Jack's recommendation, Dean Phelps instructed a fine of twenty-five dollars imposed on each offender before releasing them. They were satisfied that the fines would more than pay the marshalling wages.

One afternoon, a freight wagon pulled up to The Way Station Saloon and unloaded a piano. The tinny music, a beacon for those coming to town, echoed the street at night.

A few days later in the evening out at the Z Bar ranch, Horace Davies and Leo Sturgis were drinking whiskey out on the front porch of the house. All the hired hands were in the bunkhouse or still finishing their evening meal.

Horace Davies was a man who held no feelings or loyalty to anyone. He held no compunction for lying, stealing or murder. He held an air of superiority over all he had dealings with, and he usually convinced others to do his bidding for him without dirtying his own hands. Now he was the owner and boss of the Z Bar ranch, he expected those in his employ to do as he directed.

'Things are coming along as I planned,' Davies said. 'In a little while, Leo, I'll send the old Nickerson cowboys away with a good portion of the herd and pay them off at the railhead. We'll keep just enough cows to make this place look like a legitimate ranch without the hassle of watching over a large herd. Once that's done, we'll be rid of the cows and the men loyal to Evelyn Nickerson too.' Davies lit a cigar and sat back in his chair. 'I've got some more men coming, some of them will be in tonight.'

'Do you think we need more muscle?' Sturgis asked.

Davies grunted. 'I need a show of force so that all those around here will know who's in charge. I want the ranch to be a place for men on the run to feel secure. We would merely require a percentage of their take from the thieving they've done in exchange for safe haven from the law. We can even line them up with some good paying jobs and they can pay us a portion of whatever they are able to steal.

'All this takes a fair amount of men to oversee things. With the proper number of men, we can take control of anything that comes in and out of Crossroads. We'll impose a tax on any freight that comes in and anyone who wants to settle around here will have to deal with us first.

'Everybody has to pay his fair share. We'll provide a

protection service to those that go along with us and run off those that dissent. I intend to be friendly to the sheriff in Midland; point out to him that our men can handle any problems that come up around here and keep the peace.'

'What about the town?' Sturgis asked.

Davies shrugged a shoulder. 'The town is going to turn out to all of our liking. It'll be a place where all the men can get their drinking, gambling and whoring done close by. I've already bought control of The Way Station Saloon and Shaw's Mercantile, and fixed it so that I can govern McKinney's House as well. I need to acquire Jack's Livery and that stage depot in order to gain a handle on the comings and goings and the mail; otherwise we have no way to know which stage is carrying any worthwhile money. If we start robbing all of them, they'll send the damned army as escorts or stop running altogether. We need our own man in that depot. Bonner has to go. He could be a real pain in the butt as long as he's toying with that do the right thing according to the law attitude. He's too hard-headed to deal with reasonably. We need to get him to move on, sooner rather than later. Ideally, he will take that woman of his and leave town without a hassle.'

'You want me to take care of him?'

Davies held his hand out in a calming manner. 'In due time, Leo. I had you in mind for just such a task when I first talked to you down in El Paso. I figured you could see to a little six-gun justice if other options fail but first, a little pressure applied might be just the right

94

thing. If a few gun hawks begin to pay Mr Lightning Jack Bonner a visit, he might get the message that it is time he found a greener, more peaceful pasture elsewhere.'

'Some who thought they could take him already tried and are now residents of Crossroads's cemetery,' Sturgis said.

'Yeah, but Bonner was getting paid damn good for that trumped up fast gun contest. The whole thing was just a stunt dreamed up by the town merchants to get people to come to town and Bonner did what he said and mowed 'em all down. What I have in mind is a little different; this time the challengers stand to be on the receiving end of the money. I want you to take a trip to El Paso; pass the word there and other places that I'll pay a bounty on Bonner, say $500. No, make that $1,000 to the man who can put him away. It doesn't really matter whether any would-be gunman wins or not; the point is to pressure Bonner into leaving Crossroads.'

'And if he don't leave soon enough?'

'Let's see how things work out, Leo.'

'I can arrange things like you want. I know of some that would be interested just for the money.'

Davies took another drink of whiskey. 'You stick by me, Leo, and we'll control this whole country before long.'

The men hushed their conversation when Barry Dobsen walked past the porch on his way to the bunkhouse from the barn.

Sturgis turned to Davies. 'You think he heard anything?'

'I don't much give a damn if he did. What I just out-lined to you will be common knowledge before long anyway.'

The next morning, Jack was standing outside the livery having a third cup of coffee when Barry Dobsen rode into town and made straight for the livery. Behind his saddle were bulging saddlebacks and bedroll. Jack watched the man as he dismounted and spun reins around a hitch pole.

'Morning, Jack,' Barry offered.

'Morning, Barry,' Jack replied. 'Coffee's on if you care for a cup.'

'Sure, I could use a cup. I came to town to see Mrs Nickerson but it might be a bit early yet.'

When the two men had a full cup in his hand, Jack motioned towards Barry's horse. 'Looks like you are taking a trip.'

'Everything I own is on that horse. I've been living on the ranch for over ten years, ever since Tom Nickerson brought me here and made me the foreman. I never thought I'd see the day but as of this morning, I am no longer employed at the ranch.'

Jack looked at Barry in amazement. 'What the heck happened out there, Barry?'

Barry took a sip of coffee. 'Horace Davies and I never did see eye to eye on much. He doesn't know a lot about cattle or the running of the ranch for that matter. We have had words more than once. A few days ago, he hired three men. I ain't saying that they might not be good cowboys but they sure are kinda rough acting characters. None of the three talk much to anyone but themselves; they spend all their time sitting in the bunkhouse playing cards. Last night, he hired four more men that the ranch did not need. We got into an argument over that and then about the treatment of the old hands. He treats all hired help as servants at his calling but I guess some men will swallow their pride when the money is good.

'Davies wouldn't listen to any reasoning. He said I was through, that I could draw my pay and leave at first light. This morning Davies handed me my pay and said that the decision was final. He said a man can't go against the boss without getting his due. That I didn't fit in with the direction he had for the ranch.

'In a way I'm glad to get out from under his thumb, though I don't like what he's doing to the ranch.

'Davies sent all the old hands off with most of the herd several days ago. When I asked about the men getting their monthly pay, Davies told me to tell the men that they would get their pay at the railhead. I figure that Davies is having a cash flow problem. The ranch never was a place to get rich from, and we always had some lean times but Nickerson always managed to make the payroll. I suspect the men will get paid but most likely will not be coming back. With most of the herd disposed of, there would be no need for them to return. I don't know why he did not just send me along with them.'

'He was most likely afraid that you'd go running to Evelyn Nickerson with the news of the sale and he didn't want anyone knowing what price he sold them for,' Jack said. 'So if all the old hands are gone, who the heck is watching over what herd is left?'

Barry sighed. 'The only ones left are those two cowboys Wade Hansen and Clarence Biggs. They seem like decent men, actual cowboys, not like the gun hands that Davies has surrounded himself with.'

'Yeah, I'd say so. Now then, the names of those three layabouts happen to be Leo, Baldy and Jug?' The men's names came to Jack without forethought.

'That's them. You already know of 'em, huh?'

'I met them,' said Jack grimly. Now he knew why the three hard cases had ridden away the other night. They obviously had pre-arranged new jobs and their night-time accommodations awaiting them at the Z Bar. 'What about the four new men he hired last night, are they cowmen or more like Sturgis and the others?'

Barry frowned. 'Come to think of it, they looked kind of rough too but then again they had been travelling. When I learned of his intent to hire them, Davies and I had our falling out before the men got settled so I wasn't even introduced.'

'Sounds to me like Davies is going to rotate the entire crew.'

'It sure looks like that is what is happening.'

Jack wondered what the hell Horace Davies was up to. Buying out Cyrus McKinney was one thing but out at the Z bar, his dismissing the old crew then hiring three no-account gunmen and then four other strangers did not add up. Jack doubted that they were the type to go bounty hunting for rustlers, if that was what Davies had in mind, and Barry had said that Leo,

Baldy and Jug were lazing around the bunkhouse. He could understand Davies rotating the crew in order to put in place his own group of loyal men, even though there were good cowmen in the old crew.

In the town of Crossroads, it appeared more than likely that Davies was making some sort of greedy move for power; attempting to flex a muscle around town to put pressure on other business owners to take his offers to purchase their enterprises seriously. If that was the case, the man would stop at nothing to get into a position to control the town and its inhabitants. Once he had control then any money the town generated would eventually flow back to him and he would have things just as he wanted.

After Barry Dobsen told of his dismissal last night, he also explained what little of the tail end of a conversation that he had overheard while walking alongside the ranch house.

'Sturgis is out to get you, Jack.'

'Sturgis already made that plain to me but at least now I know who he's working for. If Davies sends Sturgis or any other want-a-be fast gun to challenge me, they'll just be digging their own graves. At some point, Davies will have to answer for what he is doing and I personally plan to see that he gets his comeuppance.'

'It sure looks like Davies is lining up the Z Bar to become his personal playgrounds and attempting to gain a foothold on Crossroads. That's a hell of far cry from what most of the folks hereabouts worked to achieve.'

'It sure appears that way to me. I don't believe he

99

gives a hoot about the residents of Crossroads or in keeping the Z Bar as a viable ranch.'

Jack tried to put all thoughts out of his mind for the moment to concentrate on the fact that here was a good man who apparently was unemployed and might be the perfect prospect for what he had in mind.

Jack turned to face Barry. 'I know you want to go over what happened with Mrs Nickerson but let me ask you this, have you ever considered becoming a lawman?'

Barry cast a sideways glance. 'You mean you'd consider me as a candidate for the marshal job being advertised?'

'That's exactly what I'm talking about, Barry. You'd be a good man for the job.'

'I hadn't considered it before Horace Davies started changing things out at the Z Bar; I'm not happy with his new ideas. I would kinda like to stick around town for a time and see what happens next. It would give me a chance to keep an eye on Mrs Nickerson's interests. If Davies were to sell part of the herd off then by rights, the money ought to go to paying off the ranch but I'm not sure of the arrangements Mrs Nickerson and her lawyer have made to that end. As far as I'm concerned, I still owe my allegiance to the Nickerson Ranch, whether I am still employed there or not.

'As far as becoming the marshal of Crossroads, I believe I could handle the job. I'm pretty good with my six-gun. I am not a quick draw, but I do OK. I'm capable of handling men and have been in a scrap or two; never backed away from a fight yet. I rode in a posse back in Austin once. Caught the men too, but I never was a town marshal or such.'

'What if you had to face off the likes of Leo, Baldy and Jug?' Jack asked.

'They put their pants on like any other man. Just because they strut around like cocks of the walk, doesn't mean that they are any good at whatever they do. With you as back-up, the two of us against them three seems like fair odds to me.'

Jack studied the man for a moment; he certainly had the grit to do the job. He let out a breath. 'OK, now that I know where you stand, I want to go talk to Dean Phelps and get his opinion on the matter while you have your talk with Mrs Nickerson.'

Jack walked to the hotel, suppressing the urge to hurry his steps. When he rapped on the office door, Dean Phelps said, 'Come in.' Then he sat back in his chair as his visitor entered.

'Morning, Jack, want some coffee?' he asked.

Jack shook his head then took a seat in the chair before the desk and got right to the purpose of the visit.

'I have a man in mind for the marshal's job,' he informed Phelps.

Phelps had a cigar in the corner of his mouth; he moved it to the other side of his mouth without using a hand. 'Why, that's a bit of good news for a change, Jack. What's his name and when can we interview this man?'

'It's Barry Dobsen. I was hoping to do the interview right away this morning, otherwise he might leave town,' Jack said.

He then told Phelps about Horace Davies having hired three gunmen, the same ones that Jack had encountered in town but a few nights ago. He told him what Barry Dobsen had related to him from the over-heard conversation.

Dean Phelps was speechless for a moment. 'Damn that Davies! It distresses me to hear that he might be exhorting a gunman to call you out. What are you going to do, Jack?'

Jack shrugged. 'I'm not one to worry over what might happen. I'll see to Sturgis or any others when and if one of them comes after me.'

Phelps grimaced. 'Maybe we should get Davies in here and let him tell us just what he has in mind.'

Jack shook his head. 'I don't believe he would show up and if he did, he would just lie and deny anything asked.'

Jack sought to get back to the intent of his visit. 'Then this morning Davies let Barry Dobsen go; the only ranch foreman that the Nickersons' ever had in favour of those three no-accounts. I suggested the marshal's job to Barry and so far, he is agreeable.'

Phelps's reaction was to say, 'I see no problem with Barry Dobsen doing the job. Hell, he's local and knows about everyone.'

'It would be a cut above having Sweeney and Roach doing what they are doing, and with Davies bringing gambling and loose women to town, it may be a wise move. I don't think that Sweeney and Roach would mind going back to being back-up assistants anyway.'

102

Phelps scratched an ear while in thought. 'I know they would like to get back to the way things were. They bitch to me every day. We'd be fools to let this man walk away. You know the saying – a bird in the hand is worth twice those in the bush. Do you think Barry understands what he would be getting into?'

'I mentioned that he might have to face those three gunmen at some point and it didn't seem to ruffle him in the least. I believe that he is ready, capable and would give it an honest effort.'

Phelps pursed his lips. 'You know what I think, Jack? I think we ought to hire the man while we can. We can find the money for wages somewhere. Hell, the way things are going, the fines imposed will be more than enough.' He smiled wickedly. 'Davies won't have any choice but to contribute to the fund since he's now a Crossroads businessman. Could be he ends up paying the marshal to go up against his own hired men. I for one would feel a whole lot better if we had this new man on our side. Who knows what Davies might pull next?'

Jack stood. 'I was hoping you'd see things in that light, Dean. As soon as Barry makes his report to Mrs Nickerson, I'll bring him in for a talk.'

When Barry Dobsen came back to the livery, he had a worried look on his face. Jack took notice.

'Things not so good at Mrs Nickerson's, Barry?'

Barry shook his head side to side. 'She wasn't happy at all. She was saddened when I told her that Davies let me go. She really got upset when I told her Davies sent off all the men and a good portion of the herd. She said she was going to send word to her lawyer. The only bright side to the conversation was when I told her about our talk on the marshal job. She was pleased with that and hoped it worked out. Evelyn and I have always been close and lately, we have been having a dinner together at least once a week. She offered me a room at her house to sleep in but I told her I didn't want tongues to wag and that I needed to be close to the job anyway, so I'd be sleeping elsewhere.'

Shortly afterwards, Jack and Barry walked into Dean Phelps's office.

When told of the responsibilities, namely keeping the peace in Crossroads, Barry said, 'I don't know much about laws that are written up.'

Jack said, 'Out here on the frontier, law isn't always applied according to how it's written up in the books. A man gets a feel for what is right and how he figures other folks ought to act. I never worried about the legality of my actions against a belligerent. A show of authority is often enough to quiet a man if he figures he might end up in the pokey.'

Barry nodded in understanding. Phelps spent a few minutes giving the prospective new marshal information on his housing and meals.

'The wage we came up with is fifty dollars a month to start with,' Phelps said.

'Plus two dollars for each fine collected,' Jack added. Phelps glared but nodded the OK.

Barry Dobsen smiled in approval. 'That seems fair.'

Jack had Barry hold his right hand up and swear an oath that he himself had taken many times before and knew the words well. Handshakes followed then Jack walked Barry over to the jail and gave him the keys.

'I have an extra set over at the livery. You can run your mount in with those in the livery corral. As soon as you are settled in, come and see me and I'll take you around town for introductions to the various business folks that make up the town, most of which you already know. Oh and there are badges in the desk drawer, you might as well start wearing one.'

Later on, Jack introduced the new marshal to several business owners in town. Most greeted Barry with an enthusiastic handshake and seemed genuinely pleased with the appointment of the new man. Willard Shaw nodded to the men but did not extend his hand. He was unsmiling as Jack and the new marshal left; perhaps Shaw was wondering how much his portion of the marshal's wages would cost him.

While having an afternoon meal at Rosa's, Jack gave a brief history of what he knew about the town and the people that made it up, in case Barry did not already know.

'As you know, I've only been here less than a year, but the town is growing.'

He retold the last bit of violence and the two hombres he had faced.

'That was the reason for hiring a marshal to start with, if I recall the meeting. I also read all about it in the papers. They had quite an article on you, Jack.'

Jack nodded. 'One of the reasons for someone else

105

to marshal this town. I don't want my past six-gun reputation to draw miscreants to town. I have retired from
law work and bounty hunting. I would like to put the
past behind me. I am now in the process of building up
my livery business. I aim to have others consider me as
a businessman who is fair in his dealings without
making my way with a six-gun.'

'Fair enough,' said Barry. 'You are retired, but if
push comes to shove?'

'Then I'll back you up,' Jack said, 'same as Sweeney
and Roach, whom you met. If you get in a bind, just call
on us.'

Jack stood. 'Time for us to venture over to The
Wayside Saloon and acquaint yourself with the new
inhabitants. I am certain that you will see a good deal
of the place come evening.'

'Have you been in there since the new people took
over?' Barry asked.

Jack shook his head. 'No need to, Sweeney and
Roach have been monitoring the place and have not
called on me for any help. I know what goes on behind
the walls. I usually do my drinking over at The
Crossroads Saloon where there are few distractions.'

The bartender at The Wayside looked up when Jack
and Barry entered; his eyes focused on the badge that
Barry was wearing. 'Afternoon, gentlemen; what's your
pleasure?'

Jack stepped to the bar. 'Just had lunch so no drinks
yet. We just came in to introduce the new town
marshal.' He held a hand towards Barry. 'This is Barry
Dobsen. You'll be seeing him around at times.'

The bartender was an older man with beady eyes and a small mouth. He was almost bald with just a half circle of brown hair around the back and sides of his ball-shaped skull. Short of height, the man pushed his round belly against the bar to lean over for a handshake.

'Glad to meet you, Marshal; I'm Eddy Kline.' He turned to face Jack and stuck out his hand to him as well.

'I'm Jack Bonner, I own Jack's Livery,' Jack said, shaking the man's damp, limp hand.

'Oh, I've heard a great deal about you, Mister Bonner, from Sweeney and Roach; I'm happy to meet you as well. Will Sweeney and Roach be continuing as the Wayside's official bouncers?'

Jack nodded. 'They will accompany the marshal in his duties tonight and will be about as needed. Now then, are there other folks who work here that the marshal should know of as well?'

Eddy motioned his head to a table in the rear where a clean-shaven, slender man with pomaded hair sat, his light-coloured jacket draped over the back of a chair. The man apparently did not note the new arrivals; he was preoccupied with dealing himself a hand of solitaire.

'Dan Lang is our resident gambler, deals an honest game, and then there are our two lovely ladies of assistance, Lulu and Ginger, but they aren't here right now, they usually come in around four o'clock for the night crowd.'

Jack studied the man for a moment. 'Your boss, Mr

107

Davies, does he come in to check on the business?'

Eddy shook his head. 'I haven't seen him but then as long as we all do our jobs, he has no reason. . . . I make the deposits every day and we keep a clean set of books. One of the men from the ranch comes by every morning and takes the accounting for review.'

'Just wondering; if he does happen to come in, can you pass along a message that I would like to speak to him?'

'Sure, no problem, Jack.'

Things were relatively quiet in Crossroads for an entire week. Barry Dobsen settled into the job. He spent most of the evening hours patrolling the street, checking doors and windows, visiting the Crossroads Saloon and answering calls to The Wayside Saloon. He was acquainted with most of the frequent saloon patrons, some of whom were cowboys formerly under his charge at the Z Bar ranch. He had quelled a number of drink-induced threats and arrested one man for firing a shot over the gambler Dan Lang's head, in an apparent dispute over a card game. When the gunshot sounded, Barry rushed to the saloon with his six-gun in hand. The shooter had his back to the batwings.

Barry called out, 'Drop the six-gun and put your hands up.'

The gunman, a new hire at the Z Bar, turned his head to face Barry but kept his six-gun pointed at Lang.

Barry called out again, 'Drop the six-gun, mister!'

The gunman sneered. 'Who says so?'

Barry stood his ground, cold-eyed. 'Can't you see that I'm wearing a badge? You violated the law by shooting that weapon in here.'

'I shoulda shot him but I didn't so I ain't done nothing to have to pay and—'

Barry cut him off. 'Shooting in a public building is reason enough to spend a night in jail. Hasn't anybody ever taken that gun of yours away before?'

The man nodded. 'One man did once.' He paused then added, 'But he died soon after.'

Barry kept his six-gun pointed menacingly towards the man. 'Either drop it or get holed.'

The man let the six-gun slip from his fingers and drop to the floor.

Another man found himself behind bars when Barry, summoned by a patron, witnessed the belligerent man slapping Ginger, one of the soiled doves, as Barry came through the batwings.

She was a woman and the chivalrous code that ingrained most western men was deeply rooted in Barry as well. He did not like to see any woman mistreated, no matter what her social status or the circumstance. In a case like this, the fine fee doubled.

When word got out that the new marshal would not put up with encumbrances, evening revellers remained loud but peaceful, perhaps in fear of facing a night in jail and a fine. The standby deputies Sweeney and Roach were available, though free from answering calls.

Lucille Rankin voiced her approval to Jack. 'Isn't this just great, Jack? Barry has taken a big burden off your shoulders and he is so capable. Evelyn Nickerson said she knew that Barry could handle the job and she is really happy for him and Crossroads.'

Jack nodded silently, though he knew a storm was brewing from the way Horace Davies was doing things. Jack did not tell Lucille about his thoughts, figuring it would only upset her. He felt that it would be only a matter of time before things turned sour.

That feeling came true one afternoon two weeks later when two men walked out of The Wayside Saloon. Instead of mounting their horses, they began a purposeful walk down the middle of the street towards the livery. Jack was readying to close up for the day, having already sent Clovis and Bobby away. He only noticed the men's approach when the taller one on the right had pulled his six-gun and checked the loads as he walked along, then put it back into the holster. The other man trudged along with a hand on the butt of his holstered six-gun. It looked as if he was talking to his partner, placing a hand to his shoulder. The man slapped the hand away then took a longer stride forward.

The one on the right had a swagger that spelled out the intent. Both men were dressed in rumpled denim trousers and cotton shirts, and low crowned, sweat-stained hats pulled low over their eyes. They held the appearance of having travelled a long trail.

Jack checked the loads in his six-gun, adding a sixth round into the chamber under the hammer. He slid the .45 in and out of the holster to loosen it, making sure the thong was clear for easy removal.

When the men got within twenty yards of the livery the man on the right called out, 'Bonner! Are you in there? It's your day of reckoning. I've come to kill you!'

The one that made the challenge was nearly thirty years old, tall, lean and lanky. Three or four day old stubble peppered his sunburned face. The other man was older but held similar features.

Jack, his right hand on his six-gun's butt, opened the door and stepped out on to the livery's low porch. He was partially shaded from the blaring sun, which was shining on the approaching men to Jack's left.

'What do you want?' Jack asked.

As if to confirm Jack's worry, the younger man said to his partner, 'We can take him, Fred, look at him. He's an old man, 'bout ready to keel over anyway.'

The middle-aged man to his right with a sprinkling of grey in his beard and hair cautioned, 'You ain't thinking straight, Clive. This old wolf is the most dangerous kind. We don't know him. It might be in our best interest to pass him by for now.'

'Shut up, Fred!' Clive snapped. 'If you ain't up to it, just move aside and watch. I'll take him on my own!'

Jack could see that behind the men, Barry Dobsen began walking towards them and was drawing his six-gun.

Unaware of the lawman's approach, Clive bent his shoulders forward, slightly hunching as he readied for the draw, his gun hand giving a slight tremor as he held it hovering over the butt of his six-gun.

'You men!' Barry Dobsen called out.

Clive either did not hear or did not care as he made

111

a move to draw his six-gun. He managed to get the nose of the barrel out of his holster when a .45 slug from Jack Bonner's six-gun slammed into the man's chest. A reflex shot from Clive's six-gun clipped the side of his own boot toe. He dropped the six-gun and stared for a moment at his wounded chest, then fell to his side gasping, 'I damned near outdrew you!'

Barry turned to Fred. 'This is the law, stand easy and keep your hands away from that weapon. I've got you covered.'

Jack walked over to stand over Clive. 'Damned near ain't good enough. You either draw first or you don't, and you didn't.'

Clive's eyes rolled; he wheezed a bloody froth then shivered as death claimed him. His legs twitched before settling to no movement.

Fred lifted his arms to shoulder height. The man did not move as Dobsen lifted his six-gun from the scarred holster.

'I believe I just saved your life, mister. Do you know who you were trying to go up against?'

Fred shook his head. 'We were given the name of Jack Bonner; s'posed to be a quick draw man but he sure as hell don't look it, he's got a spread around his middle that ain't going to do anything but get bigger.'

Barry chuckled. 'You must be new to this part of the country. The town's cemetery is home to some others who figured that same way. Let me guess, you just got hired at the Z Bar ranch and someone encouraged you to take on Jack Bonner for some reason.'

Fred grimaced. 'We spent the night out at that ranch

112

but we didn't get hired; nobody offered us a job. They fed us this morning then we left. Last night, one of the men said there was a bounty on Bonner.'

Jack stepped forward to face Fred. 'A bounty, you say; how much?'

Fred didn't say anything. Jack pulled his six-gun and cocked it. 'Nobody said you could walk away free. I have every right to shoot you down like a dog!'

'A thousand dollars is what was said.'

'Tell me about it.' Jack demanded.

'We come into town figuring to size things up if they were favourable and if not, then we'd move on. We got jobs waiting for us over in New Mexico. We had a couple of drinks and Clive decided to go ahead but I didn't like the looks of things and tried to get him to quit or at least wait. He wouldn't listen; wanted to take care of business and get the money now. I didn't have a part in this. I'm just a hard-working man trying to get along and this thing Clive was trying to do ain't making things any easier. I guess the best thing for me to do is to be on my way.'

'Not hardly,' Jack said, 'there is no lawful bounty on me, so if an illegal bounty is put out on a law enforcement official, then we need to know who offered it so they can be prosecuted.'

'We were told that you are an ex-lawman,' Fred noted sourly.

Jack grinned. 'I've been sworn in; never did swear out. Give the marshal your name and the name of your partner for the marker.'

'My name is Fred Black and his was Clive White,'

Fred replied.

'Mr Black and Mr White; real brainy names,' Jack snorted.

Fred shrugged. 'That's what they are.'

'Tell us the name of the individual who offered the bounty? It would be easier on you if you cooperated. If we've a mind to, we could hold you in custody, either here or over to the Midland jail. Makes no never mind to me how long you enjoy your stay.'

'Hell, I didn't ask the man's name that we talked to, big fella with a scar on his right cheek; said all we had to do was bring the body for identification and we'd get paid on the spot.'

'It wasn't Horace Davies, huh?' Jack asked.

'The big man said the boss was away on business.'

Jack sighed disgustedly. 'How convenient; so you'd kill a man for money, not even knowing if the bounty is legal or not?'

'It's been done before.'

'Yeah and it's called murder. Who is the money man, the one who said he would pay you?'

'I told you, we didn't get a name.'

Barry motioned the muzzle of his six-gun towards the jail. 'Let's go.'

After the prisoner was locked into a cell, Jack offered, 'I could use a drink, Barry; care to join me?'

'I ought to see that Harry Simms picks the body up and gets their horses up to the livery.'

Jack stood for a moment in thought then said, 'I think I have a better idea, Barry; one that will get somebody's attention.'

114

Barry stared at Jack, waiting for an explanation. Jack stepped out of the door and motioned for Barry to follow. Once outside, he said, 'I think we ought to load the body on to his horse and let the one that's still kicking deliver him out to the Z Bar ranch. It would be a good message to the one offering the bounty.'

'But what about holding on to Fred until he talks?' Barry asked.

'I told him that to get his reaction. If he was going to point a finger at anyone, he'd have already done so to avoid jail. We'd be better off to send him along. Keep his guns for a few days. If he wants to get them back, he'll make the delivery.'

When the body was loaded, Jack and Barry led Fred out of the jail to the waiting horses.

'You take this body out to the Z Bar and present it to the man that made you the offer. You do that and we'll let the hold we got on you slide for now. Come back three days from now and you can pick up your guns and ride on to New Mexico. If you decide to stick around, prepare for trouble because if you pull a gun on either one of us, I'll kill you; understood?'

Fred, disgruntled by having no choice in the matter, gritted his teeth and held his tongue but nodded in agreement. He mounted his horse and took the lead rope to the other horse in hand then touched a heel to his horse.

Jack and Barry watched while the man walked the animals out of town.

'I hope that gets the effect you expect, Jack,' Barry said.

115

'We'll see, now I'm going for that drink.'

He stepped away and walked to The Crossroads Saloon. Melvin Hines had a bottle and a shot glass waiting when Jack stepped to the bar.

'I heard the shots, Jack, glad to see that you are OK.'

The *Gazette* owner, Iver Faulk, came rushing into the saloon and hustled to stand beside Jack. 'Who was it you shot, Jack?'

Jack took a sip of the whiskey, grateful that it was good and strong. 'I don't rightly know his true name; was told he went by the name of Clive White. He didn't introduce himself, though.'

Iver shook his head. 'It don't really matter, I guess, but people are going to hear about it. You can't keep something like this quiet and it's likely to cause more trouble. Somebody will hear and think he ought to challenge the winner of the duel to see if he can best you. Might be just like old times.'

Jack gave Iver a baleful glance. 'I'm sure that Milton Ayers over at the *Centennial* will want all the details, Iver, and I figure you're just the man to give them to him.'

Jack raised his glass and slugged the remainder of his drink, then turned and walked out.

Lucille was petrified at the news of the shooting. She and Jack engaged in a heated exchange of words.

'Who would put a bounty out on you, Jack?'

'I wasn't given that information.'

'Didn't you ask the man's partner, the one you had Barry send away?'

'Yep, but he said he didn't know.'

'That's crazy, Jack! More men are likely to come after you. Can't you put aside your gun and let Barry handle this?'

Jack pursed his lips. 'It was Barry who saved me from being shot by the other gunman. That one could have shot me and claimed his share of the money but he chose to give up. I expect there will be others. If there is a bounty, I'm certain it does not specify that the victim be armed or not. There is not much either Barry or I can do about it until we find out who ordered the bounty. I'll pay that person a visit when I know who it is. Until then I intend to stay armed and defend myself.'

Both Lucille and Jack tired of their cross exchange then and chose to remain silent.

Two days later in the afternoon, twelve men walked their horses into Crossroads, casting wary eyes to either side of the street as they rode along. Each man had one hand holding the reins; the other held loosely near the butt of a six-gun on his side. They brought their horses to the hitch rail fronting The Wayside Saloon. The men wrapped or tied reins to the rail, stepped away from their mounts and walked through the batwings. Jack, who was inside the livery, had noticed the arrival as had Barry Dobsen, who was talking to Iver Faulk outside the *Gazette*'s office.

Barry walked to the livery.

'You noticed that group too,' Jack said as he stepped out to meet him.

Barry nodded. 'I didn't recognize any one of them.'

117

'The distance was too far for me to see,' Jack said. 'What say we wander over and make our presence known; maybe learn of their intent.'

Barry noticed when Jack loosed the thong on his six-gun. 'You expecting trouble, Jack?'

'No, but it might pay to be prepared, just in case,' Jack replied.

They heard the banter of the men inside the saloon before reaching the entrance. Jack stepped through the batwings first, Barry close behind him. A silence came over the place as all eyes were cast on the new arrivals.

Two men stood at the bar while ten others slouched in chairs with drink glasses before them. They had careful eyes and stilled hands that automatically dropped close to their holstered six-guns. They were docile now but when the need arose, they looked as if they could be as quick and deadly as a striking rattler.

Jack walked around the room, casting his eyes to any that would meet his. He knew half of them by name. Lon Riggs, little Joe Burden, Bill Crume, Joe Elias the back shooter, Steven Millard and the fastest of the bunch, Rich Tome. He'd never seen that many gun-slicks in one place at the same time other than Huntsville prison when he'd delivered Millard there some ten years ago.

'Finished your time, Steven?'

Millard nodded. 'Six months ago.'

Jack queried Lon Riggs. 'Just for the money, eh, Lon?'

Riggs slit his eyes and nodded without replying.

Jack got to Joe Elias. 'Haven't got caught up with yet, Joe?'

Joe fidgeted in his chair. 'Ain't done nothing to be on the run, Jack.'

'Back shootin' usually don't produce witnesses,' Jack snorted.

He turned and held a hand towards Barry. 'This is Marshal Barry Dobsen. He likes a quiet, clean town.'

A tall, lanky man standing at the bar, Rich Tome, spoke up. 'Glad you took the time to introduce us, Jack. We just came into town to look the town over; get acquainted, have a drink; wasn't planning on starting anything.'

'Checking things out after signing up with your new employer, I expect; seeing what you're up against. Just so's you know, it doesn't matter how much money the Z Bar is paying you, Barry and I are here to finish any-thing that just happens to get started in town.'

Tome's face flushed with anger. 'I heard you were out of it, Jack; shot down by some loud-mouthed kid a while back. Maybe age is catching up with you.'

Jack grinned. 'You heard right, Rich; I did get hit but as you can see I'm still walking around. Anytime you want to test if my age has slowed me, I'll be ready.'

He then turned and walked out with Barry.

Once out on the street Barry commented, 'You didn't seem too happy to see those men, Jack.'

Jack stopped and faced Barry. 'Best to let wolves know up front that this ain't an easy catch. They'll run over you, if you were to allow it. Sometimes a heavy hand is called for.'

119

'You think any of them will take the hint and leave?' Barry asked.

Jack shrugged. 'Maybe a wannabe or two but those long-experienced men will stick with it as long as the money keeps coming their way. Hell, it's a gravy train for them; getting paid to wait until ordered to pull their irons.'

'What do they want or intend to do?'

Jack didn't flinch. 'I suspect Davies is amassing a small army; lining them up to make a strike sooner or later. I figure that he wants to control the town and those that inhabit it. So far, he's off to a hell of a start and with no one to stand in his way but you and me.'

That night, all seemed quiet in town save for the piano music coming from The Wayside Saloon. Jack and Lucille had finished dinner and Jack helped clear the table and put away the dishes. They retired to the living room; sitting in easy chairs discussing the day's events.

It was nearly 8 p.m. and dark outside when a rifle shot blasted the calm. The bullet shattered a window then passed through to swish just over Jack's head. Jack dived to the floor.

Lucille wasted no time slipping to the floor as well, her eyes flaring. 'What was that? Are you OK, Jack?'

'Someone trying to get my attention, I believe. He missed me. Douse the lamp,' he instructed. Lucille crawled to the table holding a single lamp, and turned the wick down and out.

Jack moved in the darkened interior to the front door where his six-gun hung on a peg. He wrapped the belt around his waist then pulled the six-gun.

'Jack, I'm scared. Don't go out there!'

'You'd rather they come in here?' he said. 'Just stay down away from the doors and windows.'

Jack knew better than to step out front, so he made his way to the back door, crouched down and slipped out. Under a sliver of a moon, which provided little light, Jack crawled to the corner of the house; he took a prone position to peer around the corner in order to conceal his profile. There were but a few scrub bushes thirty yards in front of the house, otherwise the nearest place anyone could hide his self would be the livery some two hundred yards away. Open prairie land surrounded the back and sides of the house. Jack surmised that for the bullet to have come through the front window, the shooter had to have made his attempt from the bushes and he had not heard any footfalls or horse hoofs making a retreat.

Jack studied the bushes. If the shooter was still around, that would be the only place he could be. His eyes now fully accustomed to the dark, Jack spent a full ten minutes staring before he detected a lump near the thickest part of the bushes.

He positioned the muzzle of his six-gun sighted on the lump. It would be a risky shot at this distance and in the dark to boot. A slight deviation would put the bullet into the dirt short of his intended target and if he missed, the shooter could easily hone in on his position and fling lead at him. Jack took a breath, then aimed the six-gun, held it with both hands and squeezed the trigger.

Whoever was there gave an immediate yelp of pain then fired a shot in Jack's direction, the bullet thumping the side of the house. The shooter then jumped to his feet, attempting to run away but one of his legs seemed to drag and would not allow a fast movement. He hobbled along, jacking another shell into the breach of the rifle and flung another shot towards Jack's position. When Jack saw the man bring the rifle muzzle towards him, he ducked behind the safety of the building corner. As soon as the rifle fired, Jack quickly rolled away from the building then fired one, two, three shots in quick succession at the shadowy figure. The man crumpled to the ground with three fresh holes in his torso to add to the one in his leg.

Jack walked over to the downed man. He stood over the body with his six-gun pointed. He toed the inert form with his boot but there was no movement. Jack holstered his six-gun then took a match from his shirt pocket and struck it. One-handedly, he rolled the corpse over and stared into the open-eyed, dead face of the back shooter Joe Elias.

'Figures,' Jack muttered.

When Jack went back to the still darkened house, he called out before the front door, 'It's OK, Lucille, go ahead and light a lamp. I got him!'

Lucille lit a lamp and stood beside the table with one hand over her mouth. Her face blanched of colour and she appeared thoroughly upset. When Jack came through the door, she said, 'I can't live this way, Jack. All this killing going on and not knowing if you are going to be alive from one minute to the next is more than I can handle. Sooner, or later, one of those bullets is going to get you and I don't want to be a witness to it. I think we should separate. As long as you insist on wearing that gun, it'll continue to draw others to you. If you want to remain here, I'll go stay with Evelyn Nickerson or Mimi Diggins.'

'I can't put the gun up until this thing is settled,' he said flatly.

He stood in thought for a moment but his thoughts were not on repairing his standing with Lucille. He was full of rage at Joe Elias trying to bushwhack him for a bounty. It wouldn't take much for him to ride out to the Z Bar and have it out with Horace Davies or shoot anyone who got in his way. If Davies had put a bounty on his head then he ought to answer for it but with all the gun hawks that Davies had assembled, it would be suicide to ride in there alone. Jack Bonner was a calculating man and knew he would have to cool down before making a cold, well-thought out move to exact retribution.

'I'll be gone a few days to Midland to see Sheriff Hughes about what's happening here in Crossroads. There are too many oddities going on for Barry and me to handle on our own. When I come back, I'll move down to the livery. I've a good bunk there.' Jack took his hat from a peg, then turned and stepped out.

He'd taken but a few steps when Barry Dobsen came running towards him, having heard the gunfire from the other end of town. Jack explained what had transpired.

'The body is over in those bushes,' he said. 'There's

bound to be a few Z Bar men in the saloon. I think we ought to load Joe Elias's body up on to his horse and have one of the men take his carcass back to the ranch. That's where he came from and it would keep the messages going right back to them. I'll leave that to you, Barry. I'm leaving right away to go see the sheriff in Midland; see if we can get a little help before this thing blows wide open.'

Jack arrived in Midland at midday the following day. He had ridden most of the night, only stopping long enough to rest his horse and snatching a couple hours of rest for himself. He found Sheriff Willie Hughes having lunch with another man at the same restaurant that he and Hughes had dined at on one of Jack's previous visits.

When Jack approached the table, Sheriff Hughes stood and shook Jack's hand then turned and introduced the man seated with his back to Jack.

'This is US Marshal Warren Hayes out of Fort Worth.' He held his hand towards Jack. 'And this is Jack Bonner from Crossroads.'

Jack waited while the man came to his feet and turned to face Jack. It was then that Jack was able to see the US marshal's badge pinned to the man's shirtfront. He wasn't a particularly large man, being of rather short stature for a man and weighed no more than 150 pounds; the size of an average cowpuncher. He had hazel eyes set in a chiselled face and a drooping moustache. The man was sun-bronzed and had a firm grip when he and Jack shook hands.

'I didn't mean to interrupt,' Jack apologized.

Sheriff Hughes was quick to answer. 'Not at all, Jack, fact is you and Crossroads were one of the subjects of our conversation. Draw up a chair and let's talk.'

Jack sat down at the table and ordered a meal for himself.

'Looks like you had a long night. Jack,' Hughes commented.

'I spent most of it in the saddle.'

When finished with the food, the three men supped coffee and smoked.

'If you rode all night, I take it that this is more than just a social call,' Hughes said. 'Thing is, we were going to make a trip over to Crossroads to visit you on a matter of importance to all of us.'

'Yeah, a social visit would be nice but as long as there's law work to do, I guess reminiscence will have to wait. What is this matter of importance you spoke of, Willie?'

Hughes lifted a hand. 'You first. Jack, tell me of your coming.'

Jack brought Hughes up to date about the hiring of Barry Dobsen as the new marshal; the horde of new faces that now inhabited the Z Bar ranch. He mentioned the shootout with Clive White and learning from his partner Fred Black of the bounty offered on Jack's head. He then added the failed ambush by Joe Elias and listed the names of the other gun slicks now lazing around Horace Davies's Z Bar ranch.

'They gotta be up to something besides herding cattle. Fact is according to Barry, the cattle are to be

125

sold and herded off.'

'Damn, I hate to hear of a private bounty. It's almost impossible to prove a charge against the one that offers it. I think you did the right thing by sending the bodies of those men back to the source. It might slow them for a time; make them more wary but I'd bet that they won't be of a mind to give up trying again. I recognize some of the names of the hired guns you mentioned and most likely have a dodger on one or more of them.'

Jack nodded. 'As long as Horace Davies is paying easy money, they'll stick with it, figuring that one of them is bound to get lucky, I guess.'

Hughes shifted in his chair. 'The name of Horace Davies has come to my attention on another matter. A Mr Weldon Bishop who owns the stage line that runs through Crossroads to El Paso came by a few days ago. He said that six of Davies's men stopped and detained the stage on its last northbound run from Crossroads. The driver said he first thought it was a hold up but the leader of the group, some fella named Leo, told him that his employer Mr Davies had hired the men as guards to ensure that the stage went through without harassment. He made it clear that he and his men could have easily held the stage up but were there as protection.

'Leo also said that Davies intended to build a better depot for overnight stays than the current one in Crossroads. So it appears he wants to put you out of business, Jack.'

'He offered to buy me out, but I turned him down,'

Jack said.

Hughes continued. 'Weldon Bishop wanted to alert me of a strange stoppage of the stage, suspecting of some sort of future extortion; that sooner or later the line would be asked to pay for the protection of its men and stages. It made him wonder if the men would be back to do hold ups if he did not agree. I suppose that if Davies does not get what he wants, then arranging hold ups might be the next step to force Bishop's hand to switch depots. So far, Davies has not done anything illegal but by his men stopping the stage, it then becomes an implied threat that I take seriously. That was when I contacted the US Marshal service in Fort Worth and Marshal Hayes here sent me a wire and showed up just last night.'

Shaw, who had been quiet to this point, filled Jack in. 'A man going by the name of Henry Denton up in the Nebraska Territory moved into a small town called Bannock, which happened to be located at a cross-roads to the Dakota Territory and the Wyoming Territory. Any commerce coming or going west or north went right through Bannock.

'Denton bought some property there then quietly hired a number of gunmen to wreak havoc on the locals until many sold out to him on the cheap offers he made. He hired some bottom of the barrel gun hands to enforce his kind of law around town, which amounted to anyone living there paying for protection and all businesses forced to pay a percentage of their daily take. Before long, he had turned the town into a haven for any gunman on the run. They were safe from any legitimate law as long as the outlaws paid Denton a hefty percentage of whatever their jobs netted them. For those who were broke, Denton would house and feed them until such time that he would supply leads to waiting heists of which he would expect to receive a hefty percentage.'

'What happened?' Jack asked.

'There is no legitimate law enforcement in the whole region. The few bounty hunters that dared venture that far north either came back empty-handed or in some cases disappeared. One day a Cavalry company, on routine patrol, rode into town. Some of Denton's gunmen apparently thought the soldiers had come to clean up the town; they panicked and began shooting, killing one soldier. All hell broke out then and I guess it was a mighty mess before the soldiers won out. They cleaned the town out of all the miscreants, all except for their leader, Henry Denton. He, in the company of two of his top guns, somehow managed to escape capture.'

'And you think Davies might be Denton or a copycat? What makes you think that?' Jack asked.

'The letter from the sheriff up in the Llano Estacado said that Denton and his two cohorts showed up in Lubbock. Under Denton's direction, his two men robbed the bank in Lubbock soon after an unusually large deposit. Makes me think there was some sort of inside information that got out to the robbers. Anyway, Denton apparently served as a lookout and somehow managed to sneak out of town with the money when the two gunmen became involved in a street shootout.

A Lubbock deputy sheriff took a fatal bullet. One of the outlaws died from the wounds he received in the gun battle, the other one, John Reagan, surrendered when surrounded.

'Reagan now faces the rope for a robbery/murder charge. He began talking in a last ditch effort for leniency in his sentence. He isn't very happy that Denton took the money then left him and his partner to answer for the robbery gone wrong. Reagan doesn't want to swing alone and would like to get Denton into his cell for a little retribution. If the information Reagan provided proves to be true then I suppose the governor will take note, maybe commute his sentence to a life of busting up stones.

'Denton had convinced the two gun slicks that it would be the last of a string of past robberies; that he had plans to buy a ranch near Crossroads and the three could then take up where they left off back in Bannock.

'From the information received from Reagan, Henry Denton voluntarily changed his name to Horace Davies in a move to get a clean start. If this is all true then the man obviously put more than a few miles behind him from Bannock. Now it looks like he's set his sights on Crossroads to fulfil his ambition and is poised to take over.'

Jack wasn't all that surprised by the information. 'Well, do you suppose the army would be interested in getting involved again?'

Shaw shook his head from side to side. 'I've already put a feeler out to the commander over in Fort Concho and he said his command was tied up with protecting new immigrants and the trails from any Indian threat and indicated that the problem I outlined with Davies was a civilian matter. That brings you up to date and the reason for my being here.'

'Figures, here you've offered Davies to them on a platter and they decline.'

'There's more to the story yet. County lawyer Avery Bartleson, said he represents Mrs Evelyn Nickerson, came by yesterday with foreclosure papers on the Z Bar ranch. Apparently, Horace Davies recently sold off a good portion of the herd without notification to Mrs Nickerson, a violation of the purchase agreement in addition to discharging the old time employees by replacing them with new men; another violation. He was also supposed to give the proceeds of the sale to Mrs Nickerson, which he failed to do and so far has missed two of his payments to the woman. I have a copy of the agreement at my office and it clearly states everything the lawyer indicated. Mr Bartleson is anxious for me to enforce the foreclosure.'

Hughes paused for a moment then continued. 'Now you know the matter of importance I spoke of. Marshal Hayes and I were going to take two deputies and escort Mr Bartleson out to the Z Bar to give notice of the fore-closure. As the place is full of hired guns, I think we need to reassess the situation. We have an opportunity for Marshal Hayes to bring Davies to justice, as well as bust up a gang in the making. I believe that we should have a larger force to ensure compliance and make what arrests needed. I can come up with maybe half a dozen men from Midland. How do you feel about arming some of the men of Crossroads? How many would be able and willing to ride with us?'

Jack's eyes flashed. 'I, uh, need to think about it for a moment. There's more than a few that would be willing to see that those skunks leave with no place to go but away. Let me see . . . besides Barry Dobsen and myself, there are two resident handymen, Sweeney and Roach, who would go for sure. I believe Abe Wilkins, the blacksmith and Stan Oldham, the barber, would go along. The rest are softies.'

Hughes nodded. 'With the marshal's help, along with Midland's six and Crossroads's six, it might be enough of a force to get the job done. The main reason for this expedition is for me as the county sheriff to enforce the foreclosure in a lawful manner. Marshal Hayes's primary interest is to arrest Horace Davies, provided we can get our hands on the man before he figures a way to skip out again. I am hopeful that this will all take place without us having to resort to gunplay but from the information you've provided, I am sceptical. If we happened to locate some other known, wanted men in that nest, then we'll arrest them.'

Jack smiled. 'You're going to clean house then. Good, when can we get the ball rolling?'

Hughes sat for a moment in thought. 'My deputies are all out and won't be in until later today. It will take me a few hours in the morning to get everyone set to go. We can start out before noon tomorrow; make a night camp so's everyone is fresh in the morning, then

131

ride into Crossroads about noon. Will that give you enough time to get your people lined up, Jack?'

'My horse and I need rest but I can head back either late tonight or at dawn. I'll have the men ready by noon. We'll all be down to the livery and the marshal's office.'

When Lon Riggs brought the horse with the body of Joe Elias draped over the saddle to the front of the ranch house, Horace Davies and several others stepped out on to the porch.

'What the hell is this?' Horace demanded. 'Who killed him? Who said to bring the body out here?' Davies was enraged, his body shaking.

Lon Riggs shrugged. 'The marshal said that Jack Bonner was the one that shot Joe and said to have the body taken home to the Z Bar.'

Horace Davies's face turned scarlet. 'Bah! That's the second body Bonner has sent out here.' He raised the volume of his voice in anger. 'I want all of you to start earning your pay. The easy money I'm paying you to sit on your butts and drink my liquor is going to dry up! All I wanted was for someone to put a stop to Bonner before he messes up what we're doing but all I get in return is two men dead! Now that Bonner knows of the bounty, he's apt to dog us. Hell, I'm surprised he didn't bring this carcass out here himself. If he does bother to come out here, I want him shot on sight. Sturgis! Where is Leo Sturgis?'

'Right here, boss.'

Davies turned to face the man. 'You're supposed to

be one of the fastest men on the draw in west Texas. I think it's time to put you to work, Leo. How about you ride into Crossroads and take care of Bonner?'

Leo grinned. 'Nothing I'd like better and it's about time. Does that thousand dollar bounty still apply?'

'You'll be paid adequately, Leo,' Davies retorted dismissively.

Leo hesitated, casting his eyes around at nothing before settling to Horace Davies face. 'I'd like a bit of something up front in good faith. I'm not against pulling iron on any man but Bonner's reputation tends to drive the price up a little. It takes the best to do the job and that could be expensive.'

Davies did a slow burn. 'Come inside and we'll take care of that.'

'Fine,' Leo said, 'just as long as we understand each other.'

'Oh we understand each other, Leo,' Davies assured him. 'What I don't need is another failure. Take as many men as you need to get the job done.'

Leo glared at Davies. 'The men are grumbling that they haven't been paid for some time now. I'm not sure they would be helpful; most likely they'd just get in the way.'

'They'll be paid; a little performance would be helpful,' Davies said tartly.

'I can do it on my own!' Leo declared.

Davies eyed him. 'Oh you want the bragging rights that you alone took down Lightning Jack Bonner.'

'I aim to do just that.'

Leo stashed the new wad of bills in a shirt pocket

then went to saddle his horse.

It was already late evening but Leo did not waste any time and he rode into Crossroads. He found The Crossroads Saloon closed with a darkened interior, as were the rest of the businesses in town. The streets were empty except for the lights and piano music coming from The Wayside Saloon. Eddy the bartender shook his head when Leo asked, 'Has Jack Bonner been in?'

'Someone said they saw him ride out of town a few hours ago after that shootout up the street.'

Leo Sturgis figured Horace Davies would be in no mood to hear that Bonner was not even in town. Sturgis stayed at the saloon until the wee hours when the last drinker had staggered through the batwings before he reluctantly rode on back to the ranch. Early the next morning, having slept restlessly with the job of disposing of Jack Bonner on his mind, he knuckled the sleep from his eyes then left the ranch before even the cook began to stir. He figured he'd get a meal at Rosa's Café and be ready for Bonner the minute he showed his mug in town.

By early afternoon, Leo Sturgis was sitting in a chair on the porch fronting the saloon. He had been sitting there since mid-morning, rolling and smoking one cig-arette after the other until his sack of tobacco was empty. Jack Bonner had not shown his face all day and it looked as if he still was not in town. Sturgis walked past Jack's livery and then from one end of Crossroads to the other but there was no sign of Bonner. He sat watching the street when two Z Bar men rode to The

Wayside and tied their reins to a hitch pole. Sturgis was in no mood to chitchat so he stood, nodded to the two men then stepped away to go buy another sack of the makin's.

Later, Sturgis had a couple shots of whiskey at The Wayside. He waited in vain until late evening then went back to the ranch. He did not care to report to Horace Davies. If the man happened to see him and ask, all he could do is call it like it is: Bonner isn't even in town.

The next morning, Sturgis did a repeat of the day before and left the ranch early. Maybe this would be his lucky day, Bonner wouldn't stay gone from his livery business forever and the minute the old gunman showed his face, Sturgis planned on bracing him. He wouldn't give the man time to rest up from a ride and prepare himself, too bad for Bonner. Sturgis knew how irritable it was to be bothered when he was hot and dry right after a long ride. The move might cause Bonner to make a fatal mistake. He also knew that Jack Bonner was fast with a six-gun and had a long and colourful past. He'd even witnessed Bonner shooting down a young gun toter up in Ellsworth but that was some time ago. Now that Bonner had some grey in his beard, he most likely had slowed. Leo Sturgis could take him, he was almost sure of it. Almost.

The third day of Sturgis's vigilant watching started out just as the other two wasted days. It was almost becoming a routine now, getting out of his bunk before daylight, saddling his horse and making the short ride into Crossroads for coffee and breakfast at Rosa's Café. He didn't mind that so much as the woman put out a good meal and wasn't stingy on the portions. When he rode into town, he could see the lamplight coming from the window at Rosa's. He guided his horse to a hitch pole to the left of the building and tied the reins.

When Leo Sturgis walked through the front door, he wasn't prepared for the sight of Jack Bonner sitting at a table with a coffee cup in one hand and the other one beneath the table top. Sturgis was greatly surprised; Bonner had either come into town unnoticed last night or the man had just got here. No matter, at least he would put an end to Bonner today.

Sturgis dropped his hand to the butt of his six-gun.

'I'd be careful if I were you, Leo,' Jack declared, 'could be that are you covered already. I'm hungry and we can settle our differences after breakfast, if you've a mind.'

Sturgis, not knowing if Jack did have a gun pointed at him, stiffened but brought his hand up. 'Sure, Jack, there's plenty of time as you say.'

Sturgis took a table away from Jack's, seating himself so that each man had a vision of the other.

Jack finished his full meal while Sturgis sat picking at his plate, having eaten lightly. Both men sat supping coffee and smoking; Sturgis was avoiding eye contact. Jack knew Sturgis was unnerved and decided to dig at the man.

'That bounty money must be looking pretty good about now, I expect.'

Sturgis pursed his lips. 'A man's gotta do what he's gotta do.'

Jack stood and laid money on the table for his break-fast.

'Well, I've got a busy schedule today, Leo; places to go and people to see. What say we wait until full daylight? By then enough folks will be out and you get the full audience you wanted. I'll be down by the livery. Take your time, enjoy your last meal,' he said snidely. He stepped out and walked away without looking back.

Sturgis was usually the one prodding his opponent and here Bonner was doing it to him. He was fuming with rage but remained silent, knowing that he needed to settle down some before bracing Bonner. The caution of self-preservation was strong enough to override the impulse to take care of business in the immediate. If he did that, one little mistake could lead to an even bigger one and Bonner was a man he couldn't afford to make a mistake with. Sturgis, in an effort to relax, began rolling another smoke then ordered a second cup of coffee. He'd let a little time pass by, let Bonner think about it some, maybe that would throw him off a little.

The sun was on the rise in the east and high enough to have chased all the darkness away by the time Sturgis came stepping down the middle of the street towards the livery. It was still early but a few of the business owners were beginning to open their doors and sweep debris and dust off their fronting boardwalks. Heads began to turn, knowing something was up when Jack Bonner stepped out of the livery and began walking steadily towards the other man. Barry Dobsen was still sleeping after a late night of keeping things semi-quiet at The Wayside Saloon.

Jack came to a standstill at his usual thirty paces. Sturgis took three more steps before he stopped. He noticed that though it was early, Sturgis was sweating profusely, the staining at the armpits of his shirt expanding as he stood ready. Both men had their gun hands hanging loose but close to their weapons.

'You don't have to do this, Leo. You can save your own hide and ride out,' Jack offered.

Sturgis replied, 'Too late for that Jack, I already took some money.'

'All right then but that's too bad. It's all up to you.'

Jack did not move a muscle, merely stared intently at Sturgis.

'Any last words, Jack?' Sturgis asked in a last ditch effort to unnerve his opponent.

Jack Bonner remained silent. Sturgis, apprehensive and anxious to get it over with, could wait no longer. He made a move for his six-gun, making a fast draw, as fast as he had ever drawn against other opponents. His six-gun was out of the holster, cocked and the muzzle rising to level when a .45 slug entered his stomach. He was fast but not fast enough. Sturgis, staggered by the hit, reflexively pulled the trigger, the bullet hitting the dirt three feet in front of Jack Bonner. Wide-eyed, he tried to bring his six-gun to bear, but Jack shot him in the stomach again. That shot caused Sturgis to take a step back then he jack-knifed forward to land on his face.

Jack walked to Sturgis's side, kicked the man's six-gun away. He reached down and rolled Sturgis on to his back. Sturgis's eyes rolled in his head drunkenly.

'Damn, that hurts,' he gasped.

'Yeah, those belly shots are hard on the digestion. You got any message you want me to send back to Horace Davies?'

Leo Sturgis opened his mouth but the only thing that came out was a flood of blood as he gagged. His body shivered and he laid still, his eyes open in death.

Earlier that morning, Horace Davies was getting edgy. This was the third day since Leo Sturgis had said he'd take care of Jack Bonner and no word had come that anything had happened. He wondered if Sturgis had taken the $500 he had advanced him and left the country, though someone had said that Leo had slept at the ranch. He didn't know Sturgis that well and was quite aware there was no loyalty among thieves. Hell, the man could ride off at any time.

Davies called little Joe Burden aside. 'I want you to ride into Crossroads and see what's going on. Leo has been gone for two days now and hasn't taken care of Bonner yet. Leo said he didn't need any help but I'm beginning to wonder what the problem is.'

Davies watched as Burden rode away. His declaration of $1,000 as a bounty on Bonner's head had not produced the results that he had wanted. He had hoped that the pressure of some challenges to the man's six-gun would have sent Bonner packing but the man had resolve, he'd give him that. Too damned bad he had been unable to buy Bonner's gun. What he should have done, upon reflection, was to send the whole gang of miscreants he'd assembled to corner Bonner and finish him off. This waiting around for mouthy gun slicks such as Sturgis to try their hand at plugging Bonner was not working out and he didn't have any more time to waste.

If he didn't get this operation bringing some money in right away, the pay he'd promised to each man would wipe him out of cash. He'd already overheard some grumbling about not getting paid from more than one dissatisfied gunman. The whiskey, grub and lodgings, plus the fifty dollars he'd given each man when he arrived along with high promises of more later, was growing thin. After a few days of lounging around, most of the seasoned men were getting restless. These were short-fused men, loyal only to their gun and themselves. Some had travelled a long distance and expected quick results, so they would start to turn on him or move on. Davies felt that he did not have any choice; if Burden came back with word that Sturgis couldn't get the job done then it was time to put this bunch to work and that would happen today.

He did not have long to wait. It was around noon time when Davies saw Joe Burden riding in and reining up in front of the ranch house. Davies went out on to the porch, glaring at Joe when the man brought his horse to a halt.

'Sturgis got himself killed,' Joe said without dismounting.

Horace Davies's face grew red with anger. 'I expect Bonner did him in.'

'I watched the whole thing. Leo wasn't as fast as he

thought he was. Let me tell you, Bonner hasn't slowed down a bit. He's as fast as I've ever known him to be.'

'What was Bonner doing afterwards?' Davies asked.

'Him and Dobsen were talking. I didn't want them to see me, otherwise they might have wanted me to bring Leo's body back here.'

Davies grimaced. 'So much for hiring a job done. Five hundred dollars wasted.' He then yelled out in a loud voice, 'Listen up, I want everyone to gather around.'

It took a few minutes before all the men came wandering in from the bunkhouse and barn. Horace Davies stood on the elevated ranch house porch until all were standing before him.

He held a hand up to silence the murmuring. 'Joe just came in from Crossroads with the news that Bonner shot down Leo Sturgis this morning. This has gone on long enough.

'First, he guns down Clive White in a stand up fight, then Joe Elias gives a try from hiding and fails. Then Bonner has the gall to send the bodies out to the Z Bar and now he's killed Leo Sturgis. Hell, Bonner is only one man and nobody alone has been able to put him out of our way. I believe it's time you all join together to get this problem taken care of.

'I say that everyone mounts up and rides into Crossroads, and put Bonner out of business. Once Bonner is done for, there will be no one to stand in our way to take over the town.'

'What about Barry Dobsen?' someone asked.

Davies cast his eyes to the voice. 'Dispose of him. I

141

am declaring that you are the new law in Crossroads and you are all deputies.' He paused for a moment to see of any dissention. When no one objected Davies continued, 'You all know that I have an interest in Wayside Saloon, Shaw's Mercantile and The McKinney House. No need to run rough shod over them but the other businesses in town, shall we say, need to know of our influence. Make them aware that from now on a fee of ten per cent of their daily take, collected weekly, will go towards providing protection from outside influence. Afterwards, there will be free whiskey over at The Crossroads Saloon and free merchandise, tobacco, six-gun shells and such at the Crossroads Mercantile. By day's end, we'll have the town tamed and the money I promised you men will start to come in.' Davies watched to see if there were any disagreements. When none came he proclaimed, 'Then let's get ready to ride in and take care of business.'

Sixteen men scurried about getting ready. In the bunkhouse, some of the men were checking weapons for full loads and rotating the cylinders, while others in the barn busied saddling their horses and pulling the cinches tight. The men went about their chores methodically, with feelings of excitement, shunning any doubt or fear of the impending action. They were thieves and worst, ready to do what they came here to do, some plundering.

Before noon, Jack, now wearing his deputy sheriff badge, Marshal Barry Dobsen, blacksmith Abe Wilkins, and barber Stan Oldham along with Sweeney and

Roach, all assembled at the jail.

Right on schedule, Sheriff Willie Hughes, his four deputies and US Marshal Warren Hayes rode from the north the length of the street towards the jail. The lawmen passed by the undertaker's building where an occupied lone coffin was leaning against the building for display. The men cast their eyes to the face of the man inside the coffin. Leo Sturgis's features were white and one eye was half-open, the other fully open but glassy in a death stare.

When they arrived at the jail, the deputies loosened the cinches on their saddles then gave their horses water while Bonner, Hughes and Shaw shook hands and talked.

Hughes pointed down the street towards the body at the undertakers. 'Trouble already, Jack?'

'One of Horace Davies's would-be bounty hunters. I figured I'd display him for a while. It makes a clear message to others that the bounty on Jack Bonner is uncollectable.'

'Glad it turned out in your favour. Now, how do you want to handle this?'

Jack eyed Hughes. 'Well, you have a foreclosure to enforce and Marshal Hayes is out to arrest Davies. I, along with these other men from Crossroads, have assembled here to back you up, so it's your show. My personal aim is to put an end to the bounty Davies put out on me.'

Hughes said, 'Let's get everyone gathered around.' When the men moved forward, he addressed the group. 'I figure that Marshal Hayes and Deputy

143

Bonner and I should be the front line to ride in and confront Horace Davies and speak our piece. The other deputies, Marshal Dobsen and Crossroads's townsmen, can spread out behind us at a distance, out of six-gun range. Make yourself as small a target as possible and be watchful if any one of those men start shooting. Our purpose is to enforce a foreclosure of the ranch. Marshal Hayes's purpose is to arrest Horace Davies. Let's hope this can be done peacefully. Either Marshal Hayes, Deputy Bonner or I will do the talking since we all have a different reason for being here. Keep in mind that the men we face are dangerous. We won't do any shooting unless they start something and it is likely that they will.'

When they were within one mile of the ranch, Jack and the others were aware of two riders that had seen the group of lawmen approaching. They watched as the riders in the distance galloped their horses back to the ranch yard, bringing their mounts to a dust-stirring halt in front of the ranch house where many of the others had begun to gather, the reins of their horses in hand.

One of the men jumped from his saddle and rushed up the steps. Horace Davies had just stepped through the ranch house front door and on to the porch to meet the hurried rider.

'There's a dozen men headed in,' the breathless man reported to Davies, 'looks to me like they're all wearing badges!'

Davies cast a glance to the line of mounted men headed towards the ranch. 'So what?' he scoffed. 'They are intruders; the exact men we were going to deal with in town.' He turned to address the men assembling in the yard.

'But them's all lawmen!' the second rider said.

'Most likely Bonner and Dobsen are the ones wearing badges and the rest are just a bunch of townsmen talked into going along. A few shots will likely see them scatter like a covey of quail. You men ought to be glad to get a chance to throw some lead at the ones that could upset our plans. They've come to us so we can settle this here and now! Everybody take up positions and wait for my order. Remember, there's a bonus in it for the man who gets Bonner.'

Bill Crume and little Joe Burden, afoot with reins in their hands, began leading their horses back towards the barn.

'I don't like going up against badge toters,' Crume complained. 'I usually do my work out of sight of the law.'

'Me too,' Burden agreed. 'I ain't looking to end up in jail for Davies or anyone else. Besides, that measly fifty dollars he gave each of us along with what grub and whiskey he's provided ain't enough to buy my gun for promises of a payday later. Reckon I'll wait and see what happens but I ain't about to take on Bonner by myself.'

In a short time, Davies's men were taking up stations at the ranch house, the barn and bunkhouse.

From the activity the lawmen observed at a distance, it was obvious that Davies had expected trouble and was preparing.

Sheriff Hughes brought the column of lawmen to a halt then directed the men to spread out in a line, Cavalry-style on the open prairie.

By Davies's direction, half a dozen men, each with a hand on the butt of a holstered six-gun, lined themselves up on the porch, three on each side of Davies as a show of readiness to face the intruders. Four others had gone into the barn while six had decided the bunkhouse was the best fortress.

When the sheriff on the right, Jack Bonner in the middle and Marshal Hayes to Jack's left brought their horses to a stop some thirty feet before the ranch house, Horace Davies stepped to stand in the doorway while facing towards the lawmen. The back-up line consisting of Marshal Dobsen, the Midland deputies and Crossroads's townsmen spread out with rifle butts resting on their thighs. Four stayed behind Hughes, Shaw and Bonner while the others walked their horses in a wide arc facing the bunkhouse and barn where Z Bar gunmen were peeking out of windows and doors.

Jack Bonner spoke up. 'Your number one fast gun has a new home, Horace. It's a coffin.'

Davies glared defiantly. 'If Leo Sturgis is who you are speaking of, he quit me last night and I paid him off. One of the men said that Leo left here early this morning. What the man did on his own is no concern of mine,' he said unconvincingly.

'Right,' Jack snorted. 'The $500 he had in his shirt pocket will buy him a fancy funeral complete with paid for mourners. Funny thing, Horace, if he quit, as you say, he forgot to take his bedroll with him. I don't suppose it's still in the bunkhouse.'

Davies shrugged.

Jug Olsen standing next to Baldy Gibbons, Leo Sturgis's two sidekicks, stiffened and pointed a finger at Jack Bonner. 'You back shoot Leo, Bonner? Leo was the fastest I've ever seen.'

Jack grinned. 'You're looking at the man that's faster. I don't need to back shoot anyone. I gave Leo the option to ride on but he chose to ignore the offer and try my hand. No matter, he'll be buried before his stink gets too bad. Oh, and by the way, I'm available to any others wanting to test me.'

Sheriff Hughes said, 'Horace Davies or Henry Denton or whatever name you are currently using, I am Willie Hughes, Sheriff of Midland County. I have with me a legal foreclosure notice from Mrs Evelyn Nickerson. Her lawyer has demonstrated to me that the terms of the purchase agreement of the ranch have been grossly violated, which brings me and my deputies here to see that you vacate the premises without prejudice or recourse to Mrs Nickerson.'

Davies glared for a moment then said, 'I am prepared to make Mrs Nickerson an offer at a discounted amount in final settlement.'

'If she wanted a discounted settlement, she would have come to you earlier,' Hughes snorted. 'The negotiations are over. We are here to see that you and your men vacate the property immediately.'

He held a hand out towards Marshal Hayes. 'Afterwards, you are to accompany US Marshal Warren Hayes to Midland to discuss your past doings in

147

Lubbock, Texas and Bannock, Nebraska Territory. These men in your employ will be allowed to leave peaceably or—'

Hughes was cut off in mid-sentence by Horace Davies. 'I'm sure we can clear this all up in short order, Sheriff. Allow me a minute to get my copy of the agreement.' In a quick move, before any objections were voiced, Davies stepped back into the doorway while reaching a hand to Rich Tome's elbow in a move to get the man to follow him. The two men then disappeared into the darkened interior of the house and closed the door behind them.

Horace Davies faced Rich Tome. 'Leo's gone so you're number one now, Rich. Of course that means a hefty raise in pay.'

Tome, surprised by the statement, swelled with pride. He stammered, 'I'll do you right, Mr Davies.'

'Yes, I know you will,' Davies said as he patted the man on the shoulder. 'Right now we have a problem. You've got to get rid of the sheriff and those other men.'

Tome stared at Davies. 'How can we do that? There's a dozen of them out there.'

'Don't we have twenty men already standing at the ready?'

Tome nodded.

'Bonner, the sheriff and that marshal are close enough that a man could hardly miss. If someone leads the way and directs the others to shoot them down, then I'm certain those townsmen riding around would not be a problem.'

Tome gulped. 'Do you think we can get them all?'

Davies smiled wickedly. 'Why don't you get the ball rolling, Rich? Step outside, draw your six-gun and shoot Bonner off his horse. The men will all back you up. There are five good gunmen still out on the porch just waiting for an order. Some members of our crew are wanted men and that's good enough reason for them to join in. If Bonner, the sheriff and that marshal are silenced the others will most likely turn tail and run. Think about it, Rich, you'll get the $1,000 bonus for plugging Bonner.'

'We got no cover out on the porch!' Tome complained.

'Then don't let your shots go to waste,' Davies said coolly.

Rich Tome made a mistake when he opened the door; he came out with his six-gun already in his hand, a foolish move that told of his intent. He yelled to the men on the porch, 'Shoot them dow—'

Tome never finished his order because a .45 slug from Jack Bonner's six-gun slammed into his chest, not only cutting him off, but also ending any future orders from the new segundo. In a heartbeat, four of the Z Bar men on the porch went for their weapons. Jug Olsen and Baldy Gibbons both managed to get off an errant shot each before a hail of lead from the mounted lawmen sent them and two other hard cases to the porch floor.

Jack Bonner fanned his six-gun after shooting Tome and accounted for Baldy Gibbons and one other. Marshal Warren Hayes shot Jug Olsen in the chest at the same time as Jug's six-gun spouted a shot that hit Shaw in the left thigh. The hit caused Shaw to fall from his horse.

Sheriff Hughes busied himself shooting the man on the right side of the porch next to where Tome had fallen then turned his six-gun on the fifth man, Steve Millard, who tried to raise his hands when Bonner's shot had taken Tome down. He wanted no part of a suicide display for Horace Davies. His attempt was too late to stop a snap shot from Sheriff Hughes's six-gun. The bullet hit Millard's right kneecap, causing him to fall forward off the porch. Millard began screeching.

'I give up! I give up!' he hollered repeatedly.

Bonner and Hughes dived from their saddles to lie on the ground with their six-guns pointed towards the ranch house. There were no covering obstacles such as a water trough or shed for the men to take refuge behind, just bare ground. Shaw writhed on the ground with blood pumping from his leg wound.

Barry Dobsen, along with the other nine men in the back up line some thirty yards behind the front line of lawmen, spurred their horses in a move to find some shelter, the only places being the sides and backs of the barn and bunkhouse. The men had their guns readied, their eyes darting hither and thither in search for any aggressive movements.

No shots came from the barn, but fire erupted from the bunkhouse. A Midland deputy fell from his horse before he could reach safety a few yards away. He lay unmoving as his horse skittered away.

Inside the bunkhouse, a young hard case grinned

when his Winchester shot had knocked the deputy from his horse.

'I got me one!' he exclaimed to a friend on his left but in his enthusiasm, he forgot to duck. A bullet punched through his right eye, spraying hair, blood and brain matter out the other side of his head. He thudded to the floor in a heap. That action caused the five other men to frantically fire their weapons without aim through the door and window openings. They weren't used to being within the confines of a building, having done most of their crimes against society while on horseback.

Three of the deputies ended up on the side of the barn away from the bunkhouse and could not return fire but the five remaining men began pouring lead into the bunkhouse. Windows shattered, the open door bounced as lead pounded into it.

Ike Sweeney managed to get behind the bunkhouse. There was no back door so he tiptoed along one side until he came to a broken outside window. He had a double barrel, ten gauge greener shotgun with both hammers cocked. Ike kneeled below the window then eased the barrel of the shotgun high enough to stick it into the window opening, pointing towards the front and fired one barrel, then swivelled the barrel a few inches and let loose again. He ducked down before any answering shots came.

'I'm hit!' someone from inside the bunkhouse yelled out.

'I can't see!' a different voice cried.

'Hold on out there,' another voice called out, 'we're

151

done for! We got four men down. We give up!'

Barry Dobsen whistled to get the other deputies' attention, holding a hand out, palm down as a message to hold their fire.

'Throw your weapons out the door and come out with your hands up,' Barry demanded.

Through the doorway, a rifle bounced off the little porch, followed by two six-guns. One man came out with hands held high. A second man limped out with a blood soaked leg.

'Is that all?' Barry asked.

'There's four more inside, but they cain't make it,' one of the men said. 'Two are dead, that I know of. That damned greener got 'em.'

In the barn, Bill Crume turned to Joe Burden. 'Damn, those law dogs just wasted all them on the porch. Looks like Davies got himself into a fix and I ain't risking getting thrown in the pokey on his account. Hell, there's even a U.S. Marshal out there and I'm told they never give up. Even if we wiped them all out, there'd be more to come later.'

Burden nodded in agreement, as did the other two men in the barn. Apparently, the six men in the bunkhouse figured differently and had poured shots futilely at the now agitated lawmen.

The men in the barn stood by immobile as the lawmen riddled the bunkhouse and now had two of their brethren standing with their hands up.

With no more shooting going on in front of the house, Jack called to Sheriff Hughes, 'Willie, cover me while I see to the marshal.'

He waited until Hughes nodded then made his way over to see Shaw's wound. Shaw sat white-faced as he held both hands to his wounded leg. Jack took one look at the man's saturated bloody leg. He took a knife from a sheath at his waist, pinched the pants up and cut into the material. He saw what he didn't want to see, the bullet had severed an artery and a spurt of blood was pumping out of Shaw with every beat of the man's heart. Jack knew that unless he could stop the bleeding, the man would bleed to death in a short while. Working quickly, Jack stripped a bandanna from around his neck and encircled it around Shaw's leg above the wound.

'Hand me your six-gun,' he instructed Shaw, who picked the six-gun from the dirt a few inches away and held it out. Jack took the six-gun from the man's bloody hand then stuck the barrel between the bandana and Shaw's leg then began twisting it. 'We got to slow that bleeding,' he advised. 'Looks like the bullet hit an artery.' When the bleeding slowed to almost nothing, Jack stopped twisting the tourniquet. 'I'll get a patch on that until we can get you some medical help. You lie back while we take care of business.'

Jack called out to Hughes, 'I think that he'll be all right but he's going to need some medical care.' Hughes nodded. 'As soon as we get Davies out of there.' Jack scrabbled over to squat next to Hughes. 'I guess we'll have to go in to get him.'

'I expect so; watch yourself, Jack, there might be others in there.'

Both men took the time to expel empty shells from their six-guns and push new ones into the cylinders.

'Whenever you're ready, Willie,' Jack said.

Hughes called out to one of the deputies who had taken shelter next to the house. 'Clarence, see if you can cover the back of the house, in case someone tries to escape. We're going in.'

Sheriff Hughes and Jack Bonner with six-guns at the ready stepped to the porch. They were both cautious of the bloodied men lying on the porch but none moved. Jack Bonner took one side of the door blocked open by Rich Tome's body while Hughes took the other. Jack entered first, holding his six-gun before him. Hughes came in to stand beside him. Off to the left was the living room where Horace Davies sat expectantly in an easy chair while puffing a cigar. He appeared at ease and it looked as if he was attempting to pass off the just finished shootings as nothing to be concerned over. He certainly did not exhibit any remorse for the act or show any feelings towards the men in his employ that had just died.

'I'm a peaceable man, Sheriff,' he claimed. 'Those men acted without my consent. You'll get no resistance from me. My personal attorney will speak with you about the proceedings involving the ranch.'

Jack Bonner advanced with his six-gun pointed at Davies. 'Five men dead on the porch and you call that no resistance?' He stepped forward and slammed a fist to Davies's jaw. The intended vicious punch knocked Davies out cold; his rotund body slumped from the chair to the floor. Jack couldn't hold back his words.

'Only because you can't buy your way to freedom.'

Hughes put manacles on Davies's wrists where the unconscious man lay. 'If you'll watch over him, Jack, I'll see to those still in resistance.' Jack nodded with a murderous glint to his eye.

Hughes noticed, and perhaps fearful that Jack might kill the man, he said, 'We need him to stand trial, Jack.'

Sheriff Hughes stepped outside cautiously, making his way to the corner of the house so that he wasn't in the line of fire from the barn or bunkhouse then he called out, 'You Z Bar men in the barn, listen up.' He paused for a moment. 'Lay your weapons down and step out and you won't be harmed. Anyone who takes another shot is subject to arrest and these deputies will draw their fire. Horace Davies is in custody and going to jail. The Z Bar ranch is no longer your home. It is now the property of its former owner. All money and assets are confiscated. Horace Davies cannot pay you so why fight for nothing? Now come out peaceably or suffer the consequences.'

Barry Dobsen and the back-up townsmen deputies with their six-guns levelled, surrounded the four men who began to walk from the barn with hands held high. Two deputies entered the barn to make sure there were no others. The surrender brought the number to seven, counting Steven Millard, who had chosen to give up without firing a shot. Any other Z Bar gunmen assigned to patrol work and not on the immediate premises were safe. Later in the day, when they came in and learned that the man who controlled the money was gone, they would not waste any time before leaving for greener pastures.

When it was determined that Warren Hayes's injury was too severe for him to be jousted about on horseback or a wagon, Jack Bonner and two other deputies carried him inside the ranch house and put him into a bed. Stan Oldham came to the bedside to assist. He searched the house for needed items, then worked quickly to stop the bleeding before stitching Shaw's leg wounds. The bullet had gone through without hitting the bone. Jack wanted to give Shaw the best care possible so he instructed Ike Sweeney to fetch Lucille Rankin out to the ranch to see to the man's care.

Deputies also took one of their own into the house as well. When shot in the side, the deputy had fallen from his horse. The fall did more to knock him out than the bullet grazing to his side. Oldham cleaned and bandaged his wound. The immobile Steven Millard, wounded in the knee and non-aggressive, was cared for too.

Horace Davies was the only man manacled for the ride to the Crossroads Jail. The others – Bill Crume, Joe Burden and four others – rode unarmed and sandwiched between mounted deputies for the ride to town.

On the ranch, five men lay dead on the front porch, four more reposed in the bunkhouse and awaited Harry Sims, whose business suddenly took a jump.

EPILOGUE

Horace Davies, now housed in the Midland County Jail, would answer to posting a bounty on Jack Bonner, inciting men to violence and past charges for robbery and murder in Lubbock, Texas and Bannock, Nebraska. He also had to answer for attempting to swindle the Nickerson ranch from Mrs Nickerson. The two surviving men from the bunkhouse would answer to charges of firing on law enforcement. The four gunmen from the barn including Joe Burden and Bill Crume were taken to the Crossroads jail for two days but were released since they had not participated in the shootout and had since left the country. Steve Millard, his wounds tended, bought a farm wagon and drove himself away.

Within a week, the little town of Crossroads reverted to its original peacefulness prior to the havoc the tyrant Horace Davies caused to the town and community. According to the Midland County lawyer Avery Bartleson, the dealings that Horace Davies had with Evelyn Nickerson for the ranch that Davies called the Z

Bar were null and void. The ranch title was transferred back to Mrs Nickerson, the down payment Davies had made was non-refundable; giving some financial relief to Mrs Nickerson as to the amount that Davies had sold the herd for. Davies had but $2,000 on his person in addition to less than $10,000 cash found at the ranch, the remnants of the herd sales money. It became obvious that Davies had a cash flow problem and relied on his promise to pay as a viable substitute, which did not go very well to buy the services of hard case gunmen. Lawyer Bartleson put in a claim to freeze all monies until litigation could free it up to Mrs Nickerson or other claimants.

The deal on The Wayside Saloon with Cyrus McKinney became void and similarly the payment made to McKinney was non-refundable. The saloon closed down the same day that Davies went to jail. The bartender, gambler and two soiled doves formerly employed at The Wayside Saloon left on the next stage out. Cyrus McKinney, with his wife gone, begged Dean Phelps to take The McKinney House back. Phelps did so but kept the deposit McKinney had made. McKinney re-opened The Wayside to see if he could make a go of it and was sending a letter to Dixie, asking if she would return.

Barry Dobsen reluctantly quit the job as marshal of Crossroads to return to the Nickerson ranch. The move resulted in the marshalling duties being handed back to Ike Sweeney and John Crane.

Evelyn Nickerson convinced Barry to restore the ranch and herd to prior Z Bar standings. They both began sending letters out to the old hands dismissed by Davies and hoped for their return. Rumours soon spread of a budding romance between Barry and Evelyn.

Everyone in town knew that Jack Bonner did not want to be the Crossroads marshal after Barry resigned. The search for a new marshal would continue. The residents, however, knew that they could rely on Jack if the need arose.

Civilization was fine and dandy for some folks but too much of it brought problems. The citizens of Crossroads appreciated the fact that the town would most likely never be much more than what it was today, quiet and isolated, tucked away here at the edge of nowhere.

Now that all threats were gone, Jack was quite content to continue his livery business. When the image of Lucille Rankin crossed his mind, Jack gave a little shake of his head. He had not seen her since she arrived at the ranch to tend to the wounded. They had nodded greetings when Jack left, leaving Lucille and the barber to their doctoring.

A week later, after getting rid of Horace Davies and his gunnies, Jack wasn't sure of the outcome. He had tried to set down new roots and to cement relationships but had he failed? He had tried to put the violent years of his life behind him and it affected him but he did not want to live the rest of his life as a reclusive loner.

Most likely Evelyn or Barry had filled Lucille in on the details.

Jack had too much respect and affection for Lucille to ask her to forget everything and share the life of a man who lived one day at a time. A woman like Lucille deserved a husband whose life did not include violence and danger by total strangers calling him into the street. Maybe things would settle down after a time, the name and reputation of Jack Bonner possibly forgotten. Any reconciliation with Lucille would be purely up to her. He'd just have to wait and see.